"You sure like **questions, d**

"I'm only trying to get my bearings. You know, develop a feel for the town," Logan explained.

"Then ask *me*." She started to scowl, squinting against the brightness of the clear day. "I don't know how they do it where you come from, but around here we don't make friends by grilling people. You were beginning to sound like a bad cop show on TV."

"In that case, I apologize."

Becky Tate and her aunt were suspects, not clients. This job was going to be harder than he'd thought, especially when it came to keeping steady company with this attractive woman.

Books by Valerie Hansen

Love Inspired

*The Wedding Arbor #84
*The Troublesome Angel #103
*The Perfect Couple #119
*Second Chances #139
*Love One Another #154
*Blessings of the Heart #206
*Samantha's Gift #217
*Everlasting Love #270

*Serenity, Arkansas

VALERIE HANSEN

was thirty when she awoke to the presence of the Lord in her life and turned to Jesus. In the years that followed she worked with young children, both in church and secular environments. She also raised a family of her own and played foster mother to a wide assortment of furred and feathered critters.

Married to her high school sweetheart since age seventeen, she now lives in an old farmhouse she and her husband renovated with their own hands. She loves to hike the wooded hills behind the house and reflect on the marvelous turn her life has taken. Not only is she privileged to reside among the loving, accepting folks in the breathtakingly beautiful Ozark Mountains of Arkansas, she also gets to share her personal faith by telling the stories of her heart for Steeple Hill's Love Inspired line.

Life doesn't get much better than that!

Her Brother's Keeper

Valerie Hansen

Steeple
Hill®

Published by Steeple Hill Books™

STEEPLE HILL BOOKS

Steeple
Hill®

RECYCLED PAPER

ISBN 0-373-44226-2

HER BROTHER'S KEEPER

Copyright © 2005 by Valerie Whisenand

www.SteepleHill.com

Printed in U.S.A.

For we walk by faith, not by sight.

Therefore, if any man be in Christ, he is a
new creature: old things are passed away;
behold, all things are become new.

—*2 Corinthians* 5:7, 17

To Franci—your kindness, forbearance and selfless love during tremendously difficult circumstances showed all of us God's love in action.
Bless you for being you.

Prologue

Rebecca Tate leaned against the edge of the phone booth outside Serenity's only grocery store and dialed the last of the four numbers on her list. Thankfully, the name scrawled on the back of the old photograph had been very unusual. If it had been something like Jones, instead of Keringhoven, she would have been overwhelmed with choices.

Ringing began. Becky's throat tightened. She'd told herself it was silly to get so excited, yet she couldn't help anticipating success with every call.

From the time she'd been old enough to ask questions, she'd wondered about her origins, about the family she'd never known. Aunt Effie had done a wonderful job of raising her. But that didn't stop her curiosity. All Becky wanted was the truth. Effie had told her so many wild, fanciful stories about her parents, especially lately, that she couldn't tell what to believe.

She was subconsciously counting the third ring when a gruff male voice interrupted with "Hello?"

His irate tone put Becky off so much she completely forgot the polite introductory speech she'd used when she'd made her earlier calls. Instead, she launched right into her story. "Mr. Keringhoven? You don't know me, but maybe you can help. I found an old photograph. It's of a family, standing by a Christmas tree. The woman looks like me and I thought…"

"What are you calling me for?"

"Be-because there was a last name on the back of the picture. Your name. And my birthday is right before Christmas, so I thought maybe—"

The man cursed. "Who are you?"

If he'd sounded even slightly amiable she'd have told him. It was the rancor sizzling through the line that kept her from speaking frankly.

"It doesn't matter. I'm sorry to have bothered you."

"Wait!"

Becky slammed the receiver down to silence his expletives. She was trembling. If that awful person was any example of what her real family was like, she was glad Aunt Effie had been the one to take her in after she was orphaned.

The list of phone numbers she'd gleaned from a search on the Internet fluttered to the ground. Becky snatched up the paper and crumpled it into a tight ball before tossing it into the trash can next to the soda pop machine. She was done looking for relatives, distant or otherwise. If Effie wasn't going to tell her the whole truth about her parents, then she'd be satisfied with what little she did know.

Besides, if the Good Lord had wanted her to make contact with her extended family, as she'd thought when she'd first stumbled across the old photograph, she'd have succeeded. Clearly, such a reunion wasn't in God's plans. The sooner she accepted that, the better off everyone would be.

Chapter One

"She's what? Oh, dear. Hold on."

Becky covered the telephone receiver with her free hand and swiveled the desk chair to face her boss. "It's Aunt Effie, again. She's dragging a ladder out of the garage and the neighbors are worried."

Brother Fleming arched his bushy gray eyebrows and rolled his eyes. "Knowing Effie, I can certainly understand why."

"So can I. I'm sorry. I know you wanted me here to meet your friend this afternoon but I'd better run home. I'll get Effie calmed down and hurry back as soon as I can, I promise."

The portly preacher nodded. "Don't worry about it. Brother Malloy will understand. There'll be plenty of time for you two to get acquainted before I actually retire."

Grabbing her purse, Becky gave him a parting smile. "I'm going to miss you, you old softy. Who else would put up with a secretary who's always taking time off in the middle of the day?"

"Logan Malloy will," Fleming said. "I've already told him a little about your home situation. He's a good man. He'll support you—at least for the short time he's going to be here helping us out."

She'd reached the office door. "You really don't think he'll want to stay permanently? I don't see why he wouldn't."

Fred Fleming shrugged. "Brother Logan is more suited to city life. After Chicago, Serenity's bound to be too dull for him."

"Dull? This place? Not with Aunt Effie around." She patted her ample shoulder bag. "If you need me for anything, call me on my cell phone. I've got it right here."

"Better leave me the number then."

"It's on the Rolodex on your desk. Remember?" No wonder she was so good at coping with her forgetful aunt, Becky mused. In the last couple of years she'd gotten plenty of practice by looking after her absentminded boss.

He nodded sagely. "Of course, of course. Well, get going young lady. Don't worry. I'll find it."

Becky wasn't so sure. She delayed just long enough to flip through the file and tag her number with a sticky note, then hurried to the door and flung it open.

It didn't swing smoothly. There was a thud and a hesitation, followed by "Ow!"

She would have lost her balance if she hadn't had a hold on the doorknob. She saw a man's fingers curl around the outer edge of the solid oak door. Moments later, half his face peered past it, revealing one deep brown eye.

She gasped. "Oh, I'm *so* sorry."

The man stepped fully into the doorway and blocked her path. He was covering his nose with his hand but even so, she could tell this was one good-looking accident victim.

She tried to dodge past him and failed. "Please excuse me. I'm really in a hurry."

"Obviously. I'd hate to think it's always this dangerous to visit Fred."

Behind her, Becky heard her boss's exclamation of joy. "Logan! Welcome. Come in, come in. You're early, my boy."

Boy? Where? Becky's gaze traveled swiftly across the man's broad chest, checked out the shoulders of his sport coat, and sped back to his face. So, this was the Logan Malloy she'd heard so much about. Well, well! The singles classes at Serenity Chapel were sure going to fill up when the women in town got an eyeful of him.

"I'm Rebecca Tate," she said, grabbing Logan's hand and shaking it very briefly. "Pleased to meet you. I really do have to hurry. Family emergency. Fred will explain everything. Excuse me?"

Wondering how the doorway had shrunk since the last time she'd passed through, she sidled by him and hurried down the hallway.

Logan chuckled as he watched her disappear around a corner, then sobered and turned to Fred. "Was that the one? She has the right reddish hair and blue eyes."

"Yes, that's her," the older man said. "She and her aunt are the only ones I know who fit the profile you gave me."

"Does she know what we suspect?"

Brother Fleming crossed the room and quietly closed the door before he answered. "No. And I want you to promise me you'll keep it that way until you're absolutely positive. I wouldn't have gotten involved if I didn't care what happens to her."

"I told you I'd do my best."

"Do better than your best," Fred said. "She's a very special person. I don't want to see her hurt."

Logan's voice was firm. "Neither do I."

* * *

Until recently, Becky had thought her job as church secretary was perfect. She loved working for gray-haired, disorganized, gentle Brother Fleming. Except for her aunt's failing mental health, her biggest worry in life had been correcting spelling errors in the pastor's monthly newsletter, or making sure his necktie wasn't decorated with the remnants of his latest meal. There were times when the sweet old guy drove her crazy but she loved him like a father. Unfortunately, Fred had decided to retire and had invited an interim pastor to stand in for him until the church pulpit committee could find a permanent replacement.

Though she'd only seen Logan Malloy for a brief moment after smacking him in the nose with the door, there was something about him that gave her pause. He was far younger than Brother Fred. And much better looking. But it was more than that—a jittery feeling she couldn't quite explain. But one thing she *was* certain of: any woman in town under the age of ninety-nine was going to be beating down the church doors to meet the new temporary preacher.

She pulled up and parked in front of the old stone house she shared with Effie. It was small but adequate for the two of them, and the yard gave her aunt plenty of opportunity to garden. Effie's spring peonies were in full bloom, their heavy blossoms weighing down the branches till they almost touched the ground. One good Arkansas storm and those petals would fall like floral confetti.

Mercy Cosgrove was waiting at the curb, wringing her thin, withered hands, while another elderly neighbor, Thelma McEntire, sported a halo of blue plastic hair curlers and clutched a poodle against her ample, flowered blouse.

Mercy hurried around the car, pink house slippers scuffing the pavement. "Oh, Becky. I'm so glad you came. I didn't know what to do. I was gonna call the fire department till I remembered how mad Effie got the last time."

"Everything'll be fine. I'll handle it. Where is she?"

The old woman pointed a bony finger. "On the roof. See? She shinnied up that there ladder like a dumb kid. No sense at all. And at her age, too."

"Oh, my. Now I *have* seen everything."

Heart pounding, Becky shaded her eyes, paused near the base of the ladder and tried to appear calm. "Hello, up there."

"Oh, praise God!" Effie hollered like she thought she was in the front row at a tent revival. "You made it! Hallelujah!"

"That's right. I'm here. You can come down now."

"Nope. Can't. Not done yet. You get your little self up here with me, missy. I need your help."

"Me?"

Becky didn't think it would help to remind Effie how frightened she'd always been of heights. While the other kids were scaling rock piles and climbing trees, she'd stood by and watched, accepting their ridicule rather than admit her fear.

"Why don't you just come down here so we can talk?" Becky asked.

"Not till I get this baby barn swallow settled back in his nest with his brothers and sisters. He fell all the way down the chimney. You should of heard the racket he was makin'."

Glad she hadn't worn a skirt to work that morning, Becky rubbed her sweaty palms on her slacks before grabbing the sides of the ladder. She lifted one foot, put it on the bottom rung, and froze—except for the uncontrollable trembling that shook her to the core.

She swallowed hard. Scared or not, she had to climb. It was sending that conclusion from her mind to her quivering muscles that was causing the delay. Finally, she forced herself to move by concentrating on the imminent danger Effie was in.

Don't look down. Don't look down. One step at a time, she told herself. *You can do it. Oh, Lord, help me!*

Knuckles white, face flushed, head swimming, Becky finally climbed high enough to peek over the eaves. Her gray-haired aunt was perched casually on the sloping side of the shingle roof, knees drawn up, gnarled fingers cupped around the small, dark body of the swallow fledgling. She looked as relaxed as someone sitting in an easy chair.

"Please come down," Becky begged. "We can call that wild bird rehabilitation guy and let him handle this. I know I've got his number."

"I couldn't find it. Looked all over a'fore I climbed up here. Nice view, though. You can see all the way to the church. How's Brother Fred doing?"

"He's fine, Effie. He sends his regards. But he needs me back at work and I can't go until you're safe."

"I'm safer up here than lots of the places I've been in my life." She gave a throaty chuckle. "Just can't get the rain cap off the chimney so's I can see the nest good. I can hear this little guy's family, though. They've gotta be right close to the edge here."

"Then they'll still be there later," Becky reasoned. "Why don't you bring the baby over here and show me?"

"Well…" Effie started to stand.

"That's right. Upsy-daisy. I'm right here for you." Becky had no clue how she was going to get her aunt turned around and backed safely down the ladder, but at least they were making progress.

Effie reached the edge of the overhang and stopped with the toes of her worn sneakers practically touching Becky's nose. She scowled at the yard below. "I see the busybodies are all gathered. What're they starin' at, anyway? Lots of people climb ladders. Happens all the time."

"Not to me, it doesn't," Becky said with a huff of self-disgust. "Would you please come down, Aunt Effie, before I faint dead away?"

"Land sakes, I forgot about your problem with heights. Don't you fret. You just go wait with my cheering section. I'll be down directly."

"I'm not leaving you up here all alone."

"I ain't alone. I got a new pet. Remember?"

"The baby bird doesn't count. He couldn't even take care of himself."

"Oh, all right. We'll do it your way. But only 'cause I love you."

"I love you, too. That's why I'm up here."

Becky had taken a step down, making room for Effie's descent, when the old woman pointed. "Who's that?"

"Where?"

"Over there. In our driveway. Gettin' out of that fancy red car. He ain't from Serenity."

A leafy maple blocked Becky's view. "I don't have a clue. I can't see the drive from here. What difference does it make? Come on."

Instead of complying, Effie screeched, "No!" and scrambled up the roof all the way to the crest.

Becky was dumbfounded. She'd seen her aunt get upset over minor things before but she'd never seen such full-blown panic.

Forgetting her own fear, Becky was back up the ladder and had crawled out onto the roof before she had time to be scared. Staying on her knees, she followed the old woman all the way to the highest point and straddled the peak for balance.

Terror and confusion filled Effie's eyes. "Duck down behind the chimney. We don't want him to see us."

"Why not?" Becky's breathlessness was more from being up so high than from exertion.

"Don't know who he might be."

"What difference does it make? The yard is full of our friends. They'll look after us. You know that."

"Still, we'd best hide awhile."

"Why?"

"To be sure they ain't found us," the old woman said. She lowered her voice to rasp, "Don't you trust nobody, you hear? Nobody."

Becky sighed. It was happening again. Poor Effie

had been troubled with hallucinations for months. The episodes were not only becoming more frequent, but her illusions were apparently gaining strength. This was the most vivid, specific one Becky had witnessed.

"I think we'd be safer if we were both on the ground," she reasoned. "Then we could jump in my car and drive away if we wanted to."

"Wouldn't do no good. They're everywhere. I saw one of 'em in the bathroom again this mornin'. She was old and gray. Real mean lookin'. She made fun of me, too. Did everything I did."

Becky had heard that complaint before. Effie sometimes didn't recognize her own reflection. Becky hated to give up the last mirror in the house, but brushing her hair and putting on lipstick in the car on her way to work was a small price to pay for a loved one's peace of mind. As soon as she got the chance, she'd remove the door from the medicine cabinet and hide it away.

"I'll see she doesn't bother you again."

"You're a good girl." Effie patted her hand, then looked surprised. "Rebecca? What're you doing up here? Where's Flo?"

It wasn't the first time Becky had heard that name. When Effie was confused she often mentioned a Flo, or Florence.

"It's just me, Aunt Effie."

"Praise the Lord! I thought he'd got you."

"I'm fine. So are you. Nobody's going to get anybody."

Logan chose that moment to stick his head up over the edge of the roof and give a cheery "Hello."

Gasping, Effie toppled over backwards. She might have slid down the opposite side of the roof if Becky hadn't grabbed her.

"Whoa," Logan said, "I didn't mean to scare you."

"You could have fooled me." Becky pulled her frail aunt into a tight embrace and glowered at him. "What are you doing here?"

"I came to see if I could help. Fred told me where you lived and gave me the directions. I didn't think it would cause a problem."

Effie peeked at him. "Fred sent you?"

"Yes," Becky explained. "Aunt Effie, meet Brother Logan Malloy. He's the new preacher I told you about. He's going to be helping Brother Fred until the church can vote on a replacement."

"Nobody'll ever replace Fred," Effie said.

"Not in our hearts. But right now, I'll settle for letting Brother Logan help us down, won't you?"

The old woman's eyes widened. "I ain't goin' nowhere with a stranger."

"He's not a stranger. He's an old friend of Fred's.

Please? For my sake?" There were unshed tears in Becky's blue eyes.

"Well...okay," Effie said reluctantly. "But if he tries anything funny, I'll teach him not to fool with decent folks."

"He's just going to guide you onto the ladder and then steady you while you climb down. Isn't that right, Brother Malloy?"

"That's right, Miss Rebecca," he drawled, obviously trying to imitate local speech inflections and failing miserably.

Becky giggled in spite of her precarious perch. "That is the *worst* southern accent I've ever heard."

"Sorry," Logan said, "I thought it might help. Okay. I'm set. The folks on the ground are steadying the ladder so it won't slip. Let's go."

Becky was glad Effie had decided to cooperate because there was no way she could have physically forced her to. She figured she'd be doing well to convince herself it was safe to crawl back across the shingles, not to mention stand up and walk to the ladder.

Thankfully, heights didn't bother Effie. She got to her feet and, tucking the baby bird in her apron pocket, proceeded as calmly as if she were on solid ground.

Dread of making the same trip brought a fluttering to Becky's chest, a lump to her throat. She'd been balanced astride the roof ridge like a rider on an immense horse. Before Logan returned, she intended to be waiting near the ladder rather than let him see her fear. All she had to do was swing one leg over and scoot that direction. All she had to do was...move.

Hmm. Apparently, that was going to be harder to do than she'd thought. Just contemplating it made her shaking grow worse—if that were possible.

Totally disgusted with herself, Becky sighed. She was frozen to the spot like a deer mesmerized by the headlights of an oncoming car. Concern for Effie may have been enough to get her up on the roof, but she was going to need more than her own willpower to make the climb down.

She closed her eyes, intending to ask her Heavenly Father for help. Instead, she thought of the stale joke about the man sitting on his roof, praying for divine rescue from a flood. Waiting for a miracle, the man had turned away every boat that came to save him, so he eventually drowned. When he got to Heaven and questioned God about not sending help, he learned that the boats he'd rejected had been the answer to his prayers.

Becky smiled wryly. Okay. She got the picture. She was stuck on a roof, too. And Logan was her boat.

She guessed it wouldn't hurt to humor him and let him help her, just this once.

Chapter Two

Becky was still sitting in the same spot when Logan returned. He stopped at the top of the ladder, smiled and held out his hand. "Okay. Your aunt is safe. Now it's your turn."

"I, um, I have a confession to make," Becky said. "I'm scared of heights."

"No kidding. Is that why you're white as a sheet and about to shake the shingles loose?"

"You noticed."

Logan chuckled amiably. "It's pretty hard not to. What would you like me to do, sling you over my shoulder like a fireman and carry you down?"

"Only if you knock me out first," she quipped. "Being right-side-up is bad enough. I know I wouldn't like hanging upside down."

"How about a blindfold?"

She made a face. "You're just full of wonderful ideas, aren't you?"

"I try." Logan shrugged. "It's up to you. Do we do this the easy way or the hard way?"

"When it comes to heights, every way is the hard way for me. I can't budge."

"Sure you can. Instead of thinking about the whole descent at once, try focusing on one little movement. Wiggle your left foot."

"That's silly."

"So is spending the rest of your life on a roof. Humor me. Try it."

"Okay, okay," Becky said, flexing her ankle. "There. Satisfied?"

"It's a start. Now the foot on the far side of the roof. Done it? Good. Now bend your knee."

Becky could see how his method might work. Before he could give any more orders, she lifted her knee high enough to bring her leg over the crest and swung it around so she was sitting, facing him.

"You're a quick learner," Logan said, grinning. He held out his arms. "Can you scoot toward me or do I need to come up there and drag you?"

"Given those choices, I think I'd rather do it myself."

"Good for you. Okay. Come on. I'm ready."

She looked down at her formerly white, linen slacks. The knees were already ruined beyond what washing would repair. Scooting along on her rear would finish them for good. Oh, well. She could always buy more clothes. A person was given only one life to risk and if sliding was the best option then she'd slide. At least she couldn't lose her balance if she wasn't standing up.

Logan pointed to her feet. "You might want to ditch those slippery shoes first. I can't believe you came up here dressed like that."

"I wasn't planning on mountain climbing when I got ready for work this morning." She slipped her feet out of her low-heeled pumps. "There. Better?"

"Hopefully. Inch yourself over this way. Take it real slow and easy."

His warning pointed out the disparity in their relative positions. When she'd scurried onto the roof after Effie, she'd apparently traveled at an angle. Therefore, Logan and the ladder were not directly below her.

"Tell you what," Becky said. "Why don't you move over, instead?"

"I'd have to go all the way down and reposition the ladder. Are you sure that's what you want?"

"Yes."

"Okay. Don't go away."

She blew him a raspberry as his head disappeared below the level of the eaves. *Don't go away, indeed.* Brother Fred had forgotten to mention that his former seminary student had a satirical sense of humor. *Like mine,* she added, smiling slightly. Life held many funny moments if she merely looked for them and appreciated the chance to laugh.

"And this one is a dandy. Brother Fred is going to love hearing all about it." Her smile broadened. Dear Fred. She was really going to miss him. Even though he was planning to retire to a small house on Lake Norfork and had promised to visit often, work wouldn't be the same without his fond greeting every morning.

Below her, she heard banging and shouting. Effie's shrill voice rose above them all. Becky gripped her shoes in her left hand and laid her right hand flat on the roof. The gravel coating on the old shingles was so loose that some of it actually stuck to her palm.

Logan had been right. If she'd had the nerve to try to walk the roof in her dress shoes, she'd probably have slipped and fallen. Given the choice of being frightened or breaking her neck, she decided she'd rather be scared silly than dead. She did, however, wish she'd made a little better impression on her new boss, even if his tenure was going to be brief.

* * *

Logan moved the ladder and headed back up as fast as he could. Becky hadn't looked very stable when he'd left her, and he could envision her exploding into hysterics at any moment. Instead, he found her smiling when he returned. Surprised, he decided it was best to proceed quickly, before she had a chance to refocus on her fright.

"Okay. I'm set," he said. His feet and legs remained braced on the ladder, his upper torso extending above the edge of the roof. He spread his arms wide. "Come on."

"Okay," Becky said lightly.

Amazed, Logan watched her start to push off. He'd expected her to inch along, slowly and cautiously. Instead, she sailed toward him like a kid racing down a snowy hill on a sled. Her feet were headed directly for his chest. At the last second, she screamed, twisted and smacked sideways into him like a gunnysack filled with potatoes.

Her momentum pushed them both backwards. Logan was sure they were going to fall. The ladder stopped almost straight up, teetered and then crashed forward into the metal guttering, bending it flat.

Breathing a heartfelt prayer, Logan held tight to Becky and waited for the next stage of the calamity, while below, her aunt was screeching words he hadn't heard since he'd left the military.

Becky wrapped her arms around his neck. Neither of them moved. Finally, she said, "You can put me down."

"No way. I'm not letting go of you till we're on the ground."

"I can manage the ladder. Really. If you try to carry me we could both fall."

"*Now,* you think of that." He rolled his eyes. "Okay. I'm going to sit you right here. I want you to bring your feet around *slowly*. Got that?"

"Of course."

"I'll believe it when I see it," Logan muttered.

As she turned, she looked into his eyes. "Are you sure you're a preacher?"

"Yes. Why?"

"You cursed."

"I did not. What gave you that idea?"

"Something you said while I was sliding. I'd rather not repeat it."

"That was a prayer for deliverance," he explained. "I suspect I'll need a lot more of them if I hang around you and your family for very long."

The lawn looked more inviting than ever before when they finally reached it. Becky did her best to

appear unaffected by her ordeal as she gave everyone a hug, starting with Effie.

The older woman was blinking back tears when
she excused herself and retreated into the house with
Thelma and the poodle.

Becky thought about collapsing in a heap on the
grass, rolling into a ball, hugging her knees to her
chest and launching into happy hysterics. *Later,* she
thought. *Later, I'll have a good, therapeutic, hissy
fit.*

The idea of actually planning to fall apart struck
her as comical. She was not the kind of person to look
forward to periods of distress the way some people
did. Sharing joy and celebrating life was more her
style.

Logan grasped her shoulders and stared at her.
"You okay? You look kind of funny."

"Me?" Becky blinked and started to grin. "If you
think *I* look funny you should see yourself. You're a
mess. There's almost as much dirt on you as there is
on me."

Dusting off her hands, she reached out and began
to groom Logan's thick hair with her fingers, meaning only to spruce him up in the same innocent way
she would have Brother Fleming. Instead, she was
caught by a sudden awareness that this was *not* the
same as tending to her virtuous old boss. Traces of

tenderness and awe flashed briefly in Logan's expression, surprising Becky, before he stepped away.

"I'm fine," he said gruffly. "Go take care of your aunt."

She looked around at her neighbors, then back to Logan. "Not before I thank you—all of you. If everybody hadn't worked together and kept that ladder from falling over, it could have been much worse."

Starting for the front porch, she paused. "Would you all like to come in? Maybe have a glass of iced tea or lemonade? I might even be able to find a few cookies."

The neighbors made excuses and left. But Logan gave Becky a lopsided smile. "A cookie, huh? You do know how to tempt me. I have a real weakness for cookies."

"Then we'd be glad to have you stay," Becky said amiably.

"You sure it's okay? I wouldn't want to give anybody the wrong impression." He thrust his hands into his pockets and struck a nonchalant pose.

"Thelma's still inside with Aunt Effie, right?"

"Far as I know."

"Then there's no chance of a misunderstanding. If those two aren't good enough chaperones to keep the gossips at bay, nobody is." She smiled knowingly. "Thanks for thinking of my reputation, though. Brother Fred said you were used to living in the city. I'm glad you realize how rumors can get out of hand in a little place like Serenity."

"The size of the town isn't the real problem," Logan said wisely. "We have small minds in big cities, too."

"I know what you mean."

"You lived in the city? Where? Little Rock?"

"No." Becky led the way inside. "I grew up in this house. But Aunt Effie didn't. She's told me what it was like in other places. Makes me even more determined to stay put, no matter what."

"Where's she from?"

"Oh, here and there. All over, I guess. She traveled a lot when she was younger."

Logan followed his hostess down the dimly lit hallway to the kitchen. "She must have mentioned some particular places."

About to answer, Becky noticed that the two older women were seated at the kitchen table, sipping mugs of tea, while the beige poodle sat at their feet. She was surprised when her aunt butted in to answer Logan.

"That's none of your business, young man. And I'll thank you to leave my niece alone."

"Aunt Effie! Mind your manners. Brother Malloy

is going to be my boss, remember? He can't leave me alone. We'll be working together."

"I'd better go," Logan said quietly, nodding and backing away. "She's confused. I understand. We'll talk some other time, when my presence won't upset her."

Becky cast a questioning glance at her aunt, then escorted him to the front door. "I don't know what came over her just now. She's usually a real sweetheart. The doctor told me to expect mood swings. I apologize. I don't know why she was so antagonistic."

Smiling pleasantly, Logan stepped onto the porch. "Don't give it another thought. She's probably mad because she thinks I was too rough with you on the roof. I'm amazed everything turned out as well as it did."

"Me, too. Our guardian angels must have been working overtime." The agreement she'd expected wasn't forthcoming so she went on. "I love the verse that says, 'He shall give his angels charge over you.' It's in Luke, I think. Or is it in the book of Psalms?"

"Both," Logan said. "Well, I'd better hit the road. Still have an appointment to keep with Fred. He told me to tell you to take the rest of the afternoon off. Hope your aunt settles down soon."

Becky smiled as she watched him leave. Recalling what he'd said about being tempted by cookies, she broke into a broad grin. Cookies weren't the worst temptation she'd faced lately. Not by a long run.

Chapter Three

It had taken Becky longer than usual to dress for work the following morning.

The baby swallow had been turned over to the bird rehabilitation man and his phone number was posted on the refrigerator door, so she decided it was safe to wear a blouse and skirt instead of slacks. Even if another fledgling got crowded out of the mud nest plastered inside the chimney, Effie wouldn't have any reason to go back up on the roof. Then again, since when did Aunt Effie need plausible reasons for the crazy things she did?

Smiling, Becky pulled into the church parking lot. Two other cars were already there; Fred's familiar beige sedan was parked near the door and Logan's bright red convertible sat closer to the beautiful stained glass side windows. The sight of the second car made her pulse jump like a grasshopper on a sizzling summer sidewalk. She huffed. If the empty car did that to her, what was going to happen when she faced its owner?

She parked next to Fred's sedan, climbed out of her economy two-door, stood tall and paused to smooth her skirt, hoping she looked presentable.

It was silly to fuss over her appearance, she told herself. After all, Brother Logan had come here to work, not to admire her. Acknowledging that fact didn't negate her jitters one bit. As a matter of fact, the closer she got to the outer door at the rear of the church, the more nervous she became.

She paused, her hand on the knob, took a deep breath and walked in.

Her heels clicked on the tile by the door before being muted by the hall carpet. She'd heard male voices when she'd entered. Now, they were silent.

With a smile, she entered the office. Her grin broadened. Brother Fred and Logan stood side by side, smiling back at her. Fred was wearing his usual suit and tie, while Logan sported a black turtleneck beneath a brown sport jacket with leather patches at the elbows. The contrast was interesting to say the least.

"Good morning." Becky glanced at her watch. "Am I late?"

Fred was quick to reassure her. "No, no, my dear. Logan and I came in early to go over some of the duties he'll be taking on in my place."

Her brow knit. "Some? I thought he was going to sub for you all the time."

"Not exactly." Fred looked to Logan as if pleading for moral support.

"That's right," Logan said. "We'll be working together on church business for a few weeks, until I get used to the routine. Fred doesn't want his congregation to feel abandoned. You understand."

"I certainly do. No offense, but I'm going to miss him something awful." She turned away and busied herself rearranging piles of paperwork to hide the depth of her emotions.

Logan approached and perched on the edge of her desk. "How's your aunt this morning? Any more excitement?"

"Not since you saw her, but thanks for asking." Becky looked up at him with an apologetic smile. "A little prickly, wasn't she?"

"A little. Has she always been like that?"

"No. At least I don't think so. Brother Fred's known her ever since she came to Serenity. I'm sure he can tell you more about her early years. I was just a baby then."

"You've lived with her all your life? What about your parents?"

"I never knew them. They died when I was very young. Effie's the only family I have left."

"You don't say."

Becky toyed briefly with the idea of mentioning the old photograph she'd found, then decided against it. Logan wouldn't know anything about those people, and dredging up the past would only raise Effie's stress level. Someday, she might divulge her secret find to Fred, especially since the older man had always seemed so fond of her family, but she certainly wasn't going to do it with Logan present.

Looking past him, Becky smiled fondly at Brother Fred. "I left the updated list of hospitalizations and illnesses on your desk. The Landers boy went home yesterday so I crossed off his name. Other than that, I think everything is current. And you have two couples scheduled for counseling this afternoon, one at two and one at three-thirty. I'll go through the messages on the answering machine right now."

"Fine, fine."

She frowned at him. "Are you feeling all right? You look kind of peaked this morning."

"I'm just a little tired," Fred said. "Haven't been sleeping well these past few weeks. Probably nervous about retiring. I don't know what I'm going to do with all that free time."

"Knowing you, you'll find enough folks who need help to keep you occupied wherever you go," Becky said with clear affection. "You're a very special guy." Seeing Fred blush made her laugh softly. "Modest, too."

Logan was nodding. He stood. "Special doesn't even begin to describe our friend Fred. Anybody who's ever known him has been blessed beyond belief."

She looked from one man to the other and back. It was as if there was an unspoken brotherly bond between them; an invisible wall that was keeping her out. Fred had never acted withdrawn like this before. Even after his wife had passed away he'd been able to continue reaching out to others in need. So why was she suddenly getting the feeling he was hiding something from her? And what could Logan Malloy have to do with it?

Becky sat down at her desk and stared at her daily planner, focusing on nothing in particular, while her brain puzzled over the question. From their first contact she'd sensed something odd about Logan. It wasn't that he'd done or said anything wrong. It was far more subtle than that. She guessed it was partly because he lacked the same outward pastoral demeanor that was so much a part of Fred.

She knew she wasn't being fair to Logan, yet how could she help how she felt? There was definitely a reserve to him that was off-putting. Perhaps that was why Brother Fred hadn't recommended him as his permanent replacement.

Then again, maybe the real fault lay within her. She found Logan too attractive for her own good, so perhaps she was subconsciously prejudiced. That notion didn't sit well on her conscience.

She was reaching for the playback button on the answering machine when Logan covered her hand with his. "I'll take care of that for you."

"I always do it." Her skin was burning beneath his gentle touch. She pulled away. "It's no trouble, really."

"I insist." Cocking his head toward the pastor's private office he said, "I think Fred wants you to help him write a couple of letters."

"I can do that later."

Logan's hand remained on the answering machine. "Please? There isn't a whole lot I can do around here until Fred assigns me a job. I'd like to feel useful."

"Well, since you put it that way."

"Thanks." Looking satisfied, he stepped into her place behind the desk and usurped her chair as soon as she vacated it. Becky was entering Fred's office when Logan called, "And shut that door after you, will you?"

"But, we never…"

The elderly pastor met her, ushered her in, and took care of closing the door behind her.

Becky blinked in disbelief. Either something strange was going on here, or she'd been reading too many mystery novels. Maybe both.

Helping her boss with his correspondence wasn't nearly as difficult for Becky as keeping him focused on one subject at a time. Multitasking was one thing. Being addlebrained was quite another. She'd never seen poor Fred acting this bumfuzzled.

"Why don't we take a break and do some of this later?" she finally suggested.

Fred paced to the office door, opened it a crack and peeked out. He seemed to relax. "Fine idea. Looks like Logan's finished with the telephone. Why don't we see where he's gotten to? I think it's time you offered to drive him around town, don't you? Give him the grand tour? Show him Serenity the way we natives see it?"

She would have answered sooner if he'd given her a chance to squeeze a word in. When he paused long enough to take a breath, she quickly said, "I have an awful lot of work to do today, Brother Fred. The newsletter isn't ready for printing, and I still have to type Sunday's bulletin, and…"

"That can wait." Hustling her into the outer office he nervously clenched and unclenched his hands as if he were trying to decide whether to pray or dither.

Becky peered into the hallway. "I don't see Brother Malloy. I'm sure he'll be back in a minute."

"Fine, fine."

Her boss's building fretfulness was troubling. She put a steadying hand on his arm. "Look, you wait here in case he comes back before I do. I'll do a quick sweep of the church and grounds and see if I can find him. Okay?"

As she started off, Fred stopped her. "Becky?"

"Yes?"

His lips pressed into a thin line. The creases in his forehead deepened. "Never mind. Go ahead. Just hurry back."

"Are you feeling sick?"

"No. Of course not. Go on. I'll be fine."

Hesitating, she assessed the man she'd admired for so many years. Whatever was bothering him seemed less physical than mental. "Okay. Hang loose. I'll be back in a sec."

She circled the west Sunday School rooms first, checked the sanctuary proper, then swung around to the east side of the building. Through the clear border of the colorful tall glass windows she could see half of the parking lot. Logan was standing by his car with his back to her, apparently talking on a cellular phone. How silly. Fred must have forgotten to tell him he could use the office line for personal calls. They could always figure out any long distance charges and settle up when the bill came.

Glad to have located him, she pushed the release bar on the outer door and swung it open. The clattery noise of the latch preceded her greeting by a split second. Smiling, she called, "Hey, Brother Malloy! We were looking for you."

Logan spun to face her. He muttered briefly into his cell phone and quickly flipped it closed. "I thought you were working with Fred?"

"I was. We're done. He sent me to find you." She sensed his displeasure and chose to elaborate. "I guess he was worried about you, although I can't imagine why. He's been acting kind of strange lately. I hope his health isn't failing."

"He seems fine to me," Logan said, joining her and holding the door open so she could precede him into the church, "but I'll keep a close eye on him if you want."

"Would you?" Her smile grew. "He's really special."

"To you, you mean?"

"To me and to everybody else in Serenity. You'd be surprised how many folks call him who aren't even members of this church. He's always willing to help."

"I know."

They entered the offices together. Fred was waiting. "There you are! I've asked Miss Rebecca to show you around while I hold the fort here." He sent a worried glance toward the answering machine. "Were there any messages?"

"A few," Logan said. He slipped a sheet of yellow paper from the bottom of the stack, folded it and tucked it into his jacket pocket. "Nothing important. I made a list for you. It's right there, by the phone."

"Wonderful, wonderful. I'll return those calls while you're gone. Have fun, you two."

"Wait a minute," Becky said, standing her ground and staring at her boss. "I said I'd go find him. I didn't promise to do anything else. Don't you think it would be best if *you* showed him around?"

Logan chuckled wryly. "You aren't afraid to be seen with me are you? If you have a jealous boyfriend, we can always invite your aunt to come along as a chaperone."

"That's the last thing I need. We'd have no peace at all if we included Effie. It'll be hard enough to explain why I was out with you, once word gets back to her."

"You could wear a disguise," Logan teased, smiling.

"What? Dark glasses and a mustache? Think that would work?"

"Not unless you tucked that beautiful red hair of yours inside a hat. I don't think I've ever seen hair quite that color."

"It's called strawberry blonde," Becky replied. "And I didn't get it out of a bottle. It's natural."

"I don't doubt it." Logan's smile faded. He reached for her arm. "Grab your purse and let's get out of here before your boss changes his mind and makes you slave over a computer all day."

"I can think of worse things," Becky muttered.

Yeah, like getting the shivers every time you touch me. And having my heart beat so hard you can probably hear it all the way across the room. And feeling scared and thrilled—all at the same time.

Logan insisted they take his car, with the top down, so he'd have a better view. "If you don't mind."

She shrugged. "Oh, no. Not at all. No sense trying to hide the fact that I'm doing the exact opposite of what my aunt asked. Might as well cruise around in a bright red convertible, make sure everybody gets a good look at us, and be done with it."

He held the passenger door for her. "Do I detect a touch of sarcasm?"

"More than a touch," Becky answered. "I know I'm a grown woman, but I owe Aunt Effie everything. I try not to upset her, especially lately."

Logan got behind the wheel, backed out of the parking spot and turned right onto Highway 62. "Do you think her condition is getting worse?"

"I don't know. It's hard to tell. Sometimes weeks will go by where she seems so normal I'll think she's well. And then some little thing will set her off again."

"There are new medications to combat senile dementia. They came along too late to help my mother but I've kept up with the research news. Just got into the habit of paying attention, I guess."

"Your mother isn't living?"

"No. Mom died while I was away. I came home for her funeral."

"I'm so sorry. What about your father?"

"Don't have a clue. Funny. All I remember about him is the smell of his cigars. And the way my mother cried after he left us."

"When did you decide to dedicate your life to the Lord?" Glancing over at him as she spoke, Becky saw the muscles in his jaw tense.

Instead of answering, Logan pointed. "Fred told me there's only one traffic signal in town. Is this it?"

"Yes. So far, at least. Make a right."

As soon as he had turned, Becky continued, "I heard there are long-range plans to widen the highway all the way from Memphis to Branson, so maybe someday we'll need more signals. Right now, though, one is more than enough." She chuckled. "Did Fred tell you what happened when they first installed this one?"

"No. What?"

"It caused lots of accidents. Some folks had driven through this intersection all their lives and never had to stop. They tended to overlook the red light. But that wasn't the funniest thing."

"Oh?" Logan slowed the car. They were approaching a town square, complete with a courthouse in the center and small businesses facing it from all four sides.

"No. Some of these people had never driven in the city. I know it's hard to believe, but they'd never seen a real traffic light, except in the movies or on TV."

"They understood red and green for stop and go, didn't they?"

"Oh, sure. The problem was making left turns. They'd see the green light, begin their turn, look up, and be faced with the red for the cross-traffic."

Logan stared at her. "They *stopped?*"

"Bingo. Right in the middle of the intersection.

Just sat there till the light changed. I don't know how many of them got dented fenders from that little mistake but we solved the problem by sending out instructions in the utility bills."

"You're kidding!"

"Nope." She drew an imaginary X over her chest with her index finger. "That's the truth. Cross my heart."

"Amazing. Looks like I have a lot to learn."

"Not really. These people are good, kind souls who would do anything for others. They have a lot of native intelligence, you know, old-fashioned common sense even if they haven't been exposed to outside influences as much as you have. Just accept them as they are and show them the same kind of respect you'd want in return, and you'll do fine."

"Do unto others, you mean."

"Exactly. We have some retirees and transplants living here, too. Some of them stay, some go back where they came from. I think a lot depends on their attitude. If they arrive feeling superior, they usually don't last long."

"But Effie stayed."

"Yes. And I'm thankful she did. Serenity is the kind of place where I want to spend the rest of my life. I wouldn't leave here for a million dollars."

"I'm glad you're happy," Logan said solemnly.

He brightened. "So, I see the courthouse, and I made it through the tricky traffic light without getting hit. Where shall we go, next?"

Becky grinned. "Just park anywhere around here and we'll walk. My friend Belinda Randall works over at the chamber of commerce. We can start there and pick up a few brochures. Maybe even a local map, if we're lucky."

"If we're lucky?"

She laughed. "You have no idea. Up until a year or so ago, when we voted to start a 911 emergency service, most of the dirt roads around here didn't even have names. They didn't need to. Folks either gave directions in landmarks or counted mileage from the pavement. It made home visitations really interesting, especially if Brother Fred wasn't familiar with the family he was looking for and they couldn't tell us who had lived in their house generations ago. That's how we navigate half the time."

The astounded look on Logan's face made her laugh again. "You'll get used to it. Just think of us as one big happy clan. And always assume the person you're talking to is related to everybody. That way, you won't accidentally insult anybody's kin."

"Now you are kidding," he said with a raised eyebrow.

Grinning widely, Becky shook her head. She stepped out as he opened her door. "Nope. 'Fraid not. But don't worry, Brother Logan. Once you've preached a few good sermons you won't have a bit of trouble being accepted. I'm sure everyone will love you."

Becky made it as far as the curb before she realized that Logan wasn't following. She turned and stared at him. He was still standing beside his car, the color drained from his face as if he'd just seen a ghost. What could she possibly have said that would effect him so strongly?

She thought back over their conversation and wondered if it was her reference to kin, or sermons, or love that had left him so disconcerted.

Whatever the reason, she was beginning to agree with Fred's assessment of their interim preacher. Logan Malloy was too different, too citified, too out of his element, to successfully assume a pastor's role in Serenity.

Like Fred, she wanted what was best for their church members. And, like Fred, she found Logan to be good company, although she wouldn't go so far as to say they were buddies. Not yet. Nor would they ever have the chance to develop a lasting friendship if he left too soon.

Becky's breath caught. To her surprise and chagrin, she had to admit it was distressing to think about the day Logan would say his final goodbye.

She quickly cast about for logical reasons to explain those feelings and settled on gratitude. She owed the new preacher plenty. It wasn't every day a person got rescued from a slippery roof and practically carried down a ladder.

Aunt Effie would undoubtedly be thrilled to see Logan leave town ASAP, in spite of his good deed on their behalf.

Becky, on the other hand, already knew she was going to miss him. What she couldn't understand was how he'd become so important to her so quickly.

Chapter Four

Becky gave Logan her most amiable smile. "Come on. The chamber of commerce is right over there, next to the county library. You'll like Belinda. She and Paul, her husband, lived over in Cotter for awhile. I was sure glad when they decided to move back to Serenity. I missed her."

She sobered, then sighed. "I'm going to miss Brother Fred, too. He's a dear."

"He always speaks highly of you," Logan said, following.

"I love a boss who's prejudiced in my favor." Glancing back, Becky noted Logan's amused smile and felt warmth immediately flood her cheeks. "I mean, it's nice to be appreciated."

"You're lucky to have found a job where that happens."

"Luck had nothing to do with it."

"Oh?"

As Logan fell into step beside her, she wondered why she'd never noticed how narrow and confining that section of sidewalk was. If she'd been wearing her sneakers instead of dress shoes, she'd have escaped into the grass alongside rather than be forced into such close proximity with such an enigmatic man.

Her *humph,* became a soft chuckle of self-derision. Talk about ridiculous. Logan Malloy had never done or said one single thing that should make her uneasy, yet she was feeling like a nervous, infatuated teenager on her first date. So she wasn't used to being around someone who acted so reserved. So what? Lots of people weren't as open and loving as the folks she'd grown up with. It was probably normal for him to be standoffish, given his background. But a southern "good ole boy" he certainly was not!

"Did I say something funny?" he asked.

"No, no." It took Becky a few moments to recall what they'd been discussing before her mind had taken off like a wild rabbit fleeing a hungry fox. "I, uh…I don't believe in luck. At least not the way most people think of it. Actually, I believe God got me my job."

"Like a heavenly employment agency?"

Becky grinned. "Something like that, yes. I was working at the ice-cream shop. Brother Fred came in for a sundae one day and we got to talking. When he mentioned an opening in the Serenity Chapel office, I knew that was the answer to my prayers."

"If you attended his church, wouldn't you have heard about the job anyway?"

"Not necessarily. And probably not in time to apply. That's another thing you'll have to get used to around here. Very few jobs have to be advertised before they're filled. And places for rent or for sale are usually spoken for before they're even vacant. Everything is by word of mouth. It's one way the local grapevine can be useful."

Becky chuckled at his confused expression. "We even have community-wide bridal and baby showers. Nobody sends out invitations. Folks just hear about it and show up with gifts. The same goes for fund-raisers like pie suppers and charity auctions."

Logan's puzzled look deepened. "Pie *what?*"

"Suppers. It's kind of an auction, except the money bid for the pies and other donated baked goods has nothing to do with their commercial value."

"Of course not," he said with a wry smile, "that would make too much sense."

Laughing, Becky nodded. "You're absolutely right. I remember a fund-raiser last year where one pecan pie sold for almost a hundred dollars."

"Whew! I've heard pecan is a rich pie but that's unreal. I hope the buyer enjoyed it."

"I think he did get to taste one little piece." Her companion's incredulous air spurred her to further explanation. "You see, after the bids are all in and the money's been collected for whatever the special need of the day is, we all stay and eat. Everything is shared. Even the expensive stuff. Makes it more enjoyable that way, and it's all for a good cause."

"Why don't you just ask for donations and skip the extra work?"

"Where's the fun in that?"

"It would sure be faster and a lot more efficient."

"Why be in a hurry when personally participating is so rewarding?" Becky smiled up at him. "The more I get to know you, the more I suspect that living in Serenity is going to give you a terrible case of culture shock. Just remember, if you get confused, ask me or Fred to explain what's going on before you get in too deep."

"I'm not as naive as you seem to think I am."

She couldn't help but laugh at his overconfidence. "You may have been at the head of your classes in school but around here you're liable to hear folks suggest you're not rowing with both oars in the water."

"I beg your pardon?"

"You know… That's like being a couple sandwiches short of a picnic. A few squares short of a quilt? Not the sharpest pencil in the box?"

"Ah. Where I come from, we say *dumber than dirt*."

Becky started across the street to the chamber of commerce office, noting that Logan had placed his hand on the small of her back to guide her safely through the intersection. His touch was barely there, yet it sent such an unexpected shiver of awareness zigzagging up her spine she figured she was lucky to remember what they were discussing, let alone come up with a lucid reply.

"Southerners are much kinder than that," she said. "We don't often resort to terms like *dumb* or *stupid*. Instead, we keep hinting at the problem till you get the idea."

"I'd much rather be told directly if I'm doing something wrong," Logan said.

She turned her head and settled her gaze on his face, trying to decide whether or not he was serious. A smile lifted one corner of her mouth. Her eyes twinkled. Her cheeks suddenly burned. "Well, if you insist. I think it would be best for both our reputations if you took your hand off my back."

Logan jumped away like a man who'd stuck his finger in an electrical socket and gotten a serious jolt. "Sorry. It was just a natural reaction. I didn't mean anything by it."

Becky's smile evened out and she nodded. "I was hoping you were trying to keep me from being run over—assuming there had been traffic in the street when we crossed."

"There was. There had to be." He looked sheepishly left and right. "There wasn't, was there?"

"Nope," Becky said with a giggle. "Nary a car. But don't worry. I'm sure not more than two or three gossips saw us. At that rate, it'll be hours before the news reaches Aunt Effie, so I'll have time to ask Brother Fred to explain everything to her."

Logan studied her expression. "You're not joking, are you?"

"Oh, no," Becky drawled, slowly shaking her head. "I wish I were."

Logan held the heavy glass door for Becky, then followed her inside. The Serenity chamber of commerce was so generic it was practically a caricature. Whoever had set up the office had obviously intended it to mirror big-city life, complete with austere chrome furnishings and a long, uninviting counter. The room looked as out of place in the quaint old town as he felt.

A young woman with dark hair greeted them warmly and came around the counter, her arms open. "Becky, hello. Who's your friend?"

Becky gave her a hug, then stepped back to say, "Belinda Randall, meet Logan Malloy. Brother Malloy is taking Brother Fred's place for the time being." Smiling, she gestured toward Logan. "I'm trying to explain small town life to Brother Malloy. I thought maybe you could give him some brochures? Maps of the area? You know, whatever you have handy."

"Gladly." The slightly older woman shook Logan's hand. "It's easy to see you're not from around here."

"Oh? Why?" One dark eyebrow arched and a smile began to quirk at the corners of his mouth. "Are you trying to tell me I'm missing a pizza—or something like that?"

Becky stared, first at him, then at her old friend, before she burst into laughter. "No, no. That was a picnic, not a pizza."

"Oh, right. I don't have enough food for the picnic. Now I remember." He knew he didn't have to explain that he was teasing. Her amusement was evident. Her friend, however, looked totally at a loss.

The chamber representative cleared her throat. "I was referring to your lack of a baseball cap. None of the local men would come to town without some kind of hat."

Logan looked to Becky. "Hey. You were supposed to help me fit in. How come you didn't tell me?"

That generated another nervous giggle. "Sorry."

"You should be. How can my mission here be taken seriously if I don't look the part? Am I supposed to wear this special headgear all the time or can I take it off to sleep?"

Chortling, Becky thumped him playfully in the shoulder. "Stop that. Poor Belinda is going to think you're as dumb as a box of rocks."

"Hey. I thought you gracious southerners didn't call people names."

"I'm ready to make an exception in your case," she told him, grinning broadly. "Grab some brochures to take with us and let's go. There's a lot more of Serenity to see."

Logan paused long enough to cause her to glance back at him. Feigning hurt feelings, he said, "Not till you get me the right kind of hat." It pleased him to see the sparkle of glee in her eyes, to hear her lighthearted laughter, to know he had been the reason for her joy.

That conclusion surprised and sobered him. He made it a rule to never become emotionally involved in his cases, especially those on the negative side. Rebecca Tate and her aunt were suspects, not clients. By the time his work in Serenity was finished, he might have brought her more sorrow than she'd ever felt before, made her hate the sight of him. If he let himself care what she thought, he'd be doing everyone a disservice.

Logan's jaw muscles clenched as the truth dawned. It was already too late. He'd started to like the very person whose quiet life he was probably going to destroy.

He steeled himself for the job ahead and forced a smile. "So, Mrs. Randall, how long have you known Rebecca? She tells me she's lived here since she was a baby. I suppose you could tell lots of interesting stories about her childhood."

"A few."

"That aunt of hers is quite a character, isn't she? Has she always been so odd?"

"Well…"

Becky interrupted. "I don't think it's right to put Aunt Effie down just because she's getting senile." She snatched up a tan baseball cap with "Spring River Country" printed on the front and smacked it into Logan's chest with more force than she'd intended.

All he said was "Ooof."

Grabbing his arm, she bid Belinda Randall goodbye as she hurried him out of the chamber office and back into the sunshine.

He resisted mildly. "What's the rush? I was just getting acquainted with your friend."

"I know. You sure like to ask a lot of personal questions, don't you?"

"I'm only trying to get my bearings. You know, develop a feel for the town."

"Then ask *me*." She started to scowl, squinting against the brightness of the clear day. "I don't know how they do it where you come from, but around here we don't make friends by grilling people. You were beginning to sound like a bad cop show on TV."

"In that case, I apologize."

As they moved toward the street, Logan started to put his hand on her back again. He stopped himself before he'd actually touched her. This job was going to be harder than he'd thought, especially when it came to keeping steady company with this attractive young woman.

He didn't know if the temptation to develop a fondness for her would feel less threatening if he were a practicing clergyman, but for the first time in years, he wished he'd gotten more on-the-job experience after his ordination.

He could also use a big dose of divine deliverance, he decided. And the sooner, the better.

Becky watched Logan surreptitiously while keeping up a patter of conversation pertaining to Serenity's history. Anything to mask her nervousness.

"A hill west of here was the site of a battle in the War Between the States. Where you come from they probably call it the Civil War." She paused for a settling breath. "Where *do* you come from, anyway? Fred mentioned Chicago. Is that where you grew up?"

"No. Fred and I met at Seminary. He was one of my professors."

"I know that. Where are your roots? You told me your mother passed away. Don't you have anybody else?"

"No."

She sighed. "I don't, either. Aunt Effie's my whole family. Of course, given her present condition, she's plenty, poor thing."

"You should look into that medication I mentioned."

"I will. Next time she sees Dr. Barryman I'll ask him about it. I imagine it works for some and not for others, depending on the cause of their illness. Being so new, it's probably really expensive."

"Is that a problem for you?"

"We're not destitute, if that's what you're asking. Effie has her Social Security and Medicare and I do as much as I can. I'll get her whatever she needs."

"The church has a fund for that kind of shortfall, doesn't it?"

"That money is for folks who really need it."

"Then let me contribute."

Becky stared at him, incredulous. "Why would you offer to do that?"

"Altruism?"

"Oh?" Her gaze narrowed, her mind in a spin. Why, with all the faith-based answers he could have given, had he chosen such a secular one?

That thought led her further into doubt. Brother Fred often expressed himself in relation to God's work or Jesus' teachings, while Logan had yet to do so. Either that was odd or she'd been hanging around a traditional pastor and living in the Bible Belt for too long. Maybe both.

Becky shook her head slowly, thoughtfully, and chanced a sidelong glance at Logan. Something was wrong. She felt as if her spirit was warning her to keep Logan Malloy at arm's length, just like Effie had wanted her to do.

Maybe that was the crux of the problem. Maybe Effie's distrust of anyone new, especially men, was catching, like the common cold. The silly notion made her smile.

Waving his hand in front of her face to disrupt her glassy-eyed stare, Logan said, "You look pretty pleased all of a sudden. I was starting to wonder if my offer of help had offended you."

"I'm sorry. No. I'm not offended. Just a little surprised, that's all. Effie and I will be fine. We always manage. Thanks, anyway."

"What did your aunt do for a living? Teach? Run a preschool program? Maybe baby sit?"

"Goodness, no. She worked in the old shirt factory over in Salem till it closed down a few years back. Aunt Effie is the *last* person anyone would want to watch their children. She's much too high-strung. Always has been. By the time I was old enough for kindergarten, I already felt like the only grown-up in my family."

"Really? If she was that flighty, I'm surprised the courts gave you to her. Must have taken a real battle to convince a judge she was capable."

"I suppose so. She's never talked about it. I assume we wound up together because she was the only relative I had left." Becky chuckled softly. "You should have heard the stories she used to tell me."

"Like what?"

"My favorite was the one about my grandmother being a princess who had fled to America to escape a forced marriage. That made my mama a princess by birth—at least half of one—and therefore I was supposedly one-quarter royalty. It's silly, I know, but it fit a child's dreams and it made me feel better about myself."

"You don't seem to have any problems with your self-image these days."

"I can't thank Effie for that. Until I realized that God loved and accepted me, faults and all, I wasn't nearly this happy. I don't mean I was miserable. Far from it. I just needed my faith in order to blossom." She smiled at him. "But what am I preaching to you for? You already know all that."

"Sure do."

Even though he had readily agreed with her, she was put off by his averted glance, his quickening steps, the stiff set of his shoulders. Looking after him, Becky wondered how a man who was supposed to be empathetic to a congregation could do his job successfully when he obviously held back so much of himself.

Weary and worried, she wished she were back at her desk dealing with lovable, bumfuzzled Brother Fred instead of traipsing all over town in the company of a man whose true nature was so difficult to fathom. For some reason, she felt as if Logan was keeping things from her. No matter how illogical that idea was, she couldn't seem to shake it.

She shivered. This was going to be a *very* long day. Thankfully, her work week was almost over. Sunday couldn't come any too soon to suit her.

Chapter Five

They stopped for lunch at Bea's Café on the north side of the square. Opening the door and taking in all the wonderful aromas was a treat in itself. The place was small, welcoming and decorated with mostly western-style memorabilia. It was also crowded—as usual.

Responding to hellos, nods of greeting and smiles from nearly everyone, Becky led the way to the only empty table and chose the side that would allow Logan to observe the room when he sat across from her. He removed his cap, even though no other male in the place had bothered to do the same.

Becky noticed his perplexity. "Around here, we have hats-on places and hats-off places. This is a hats-on place. It just means it's very informal."

"I see that. How will I know which is which?"

"The best way is by observation. Like now."

Logan was fingering the stiff brim of his new cap. "I feel like I ought to put it back on so everybody won't stare, but that goes against the way I was brought up."

"Look at this as ultracasual dining," she said with a smile. "Imagine you're at a tailgate party or a picnic and then do as you please. Be comfortable."

"Comfortable? I feel like I'm on a different planet." One corner of his mouth quirked. "And I'm definitely the alien around here. Nobody's paid this much attention to me since I was assigned to foot patrols overseas."

"Excuse me?"

"In the army," Logan explained. "That's why I was away when my mother was failing. Didn't Fred tell you?"

"No. He never said a word about that. Were you a chaplain?"

Logan shook his head, his eyes on the menu instead of his companion. "No."

Although it struck Becky as odd that an ordained clergyman wouldn't follow his chosen profession, even in the military, she didn't comment. What Logan might have done in the past was none of her business, no more than Effie's background was any concern of his. Curiosity wasn't enough to make her ask for details when he obviously didn't want to share them. There was no hurry. She could always quiz Fred about Logan later if she wanted.

"The catfish dinner is very good here," Becky said. "And the hushpuppies are to die for."

"Are those like French fries?"

She giggled. "Oh, brother, you do have a lot to learn, don't you?"

"*Now* what did I say?"

"Nothing. Do yourself a favor and keep your mouth shut till you get used to living around here."

"Must be awfully hard to eat that way."

Chuckling at his silly comment she leaned across the small table to speak more privately. "Half the people in here go to our church and the rest know me from other places. If you want to do Fred a real favor, you'll stop talking like a Yankee who accidentally wandered too far south."

Logan's brow knit. "I did that?"

"*Oh, yes.* For your information, hushpuppies are little fried balls of cornmeal batter. We always eat them with catfish. That, and pickled green tomatoes." Becky leaned back, folded her hands in her lap and smiled. "Just relax and let me order for both of us."

"Suits me. I lived on army chow for three years. I can eat anything."

"I really admire the people in our armed forces. Would you like to tell me more?"

His brow furrowed again. His eyes narrowed. All he said was "No."

That answer was getting far too familiar to suit Becky. If Logan Malloy *wasn't* hiding something, he was certainly giving a good impression of someone who *was*. Honesty and openness were qualities anyone would expect from a man in his profession, so why was he holding back so much of himself? It didn't make any sense.

Logan wiped his mouth and fingers with his napkin and leaned back from the table. "Those little dough balls sure were good. Why in the world are they named after dogs?"

"In the old days folks used to fry up little dabs of batter to toss to their puppies to keep them from begging and whining for food. That's supposedly where the name came from. I kind of doubt they were seasoned like these. They were probably more like corn dodgers."

She could tell from his confused look that she'd lost him again. "Those are kind of like cornbread cookies. You do know what cornbread is, don't you?"

"Of course."

"That's a relief. I was beginning to wonder if we were ever going to find common ground."

As she watched, Logan's amiable expression changed and became unreadable. It was as if he were closing himself off from her, from everything around them. Why? Her conversation had been meant as friendly banter, not ridicule. Was it possible that the man was not only unfamiliar with southern customs and cuisine, but he also lacked the ability to appreciate her easygoing sense of humor? If so, she felt sorry for him. No one should have to go through life so somber.

She thought of Fred, with his bumbling ways and loving heart. That man had gone through more earthly trials than anyone else she knew, yet he always managed to find reasons to give praise and lift everyone's spirits, including his own.

Becky thumbed the bill off the edge of the table and reached for her purse. "I'm going to go order take-out for Brother Fred. You stay here and finish eating. I'll be right back."

Before Logan could stand, let alone object, she'd hurried off. He watched her zigzag between the tables and head for the counter. Right age, right build, right hair and eyes. She had to be the one he was looking for. Only she was sure no baby anymore.

Becky stopped to speak to the waitress, a middle-aged woman who'd been introduced as the original Bea of Bea's Café, giving Logan a few moments in which to gather his thoughts and relive the past few minutes. When Becky had mentioned finding common ground, he'd nearly choked on his iced tea. She and he had plenty in common already, and if his theories were correct, it was mostly bad—especially for Rebecca Tate and her aunt.

Still, it was his job to dig deep enough to ferret out the truth, for his client's sake, and that was exactly what he intended to do, whether he liked this assignment or not.

Muttering to himself, Logan pushed away from the table and put on his cap. Not *like* this assignment? Hah! He hated it. He'd already started to admire Rebecca far too much for his own good. And he was ninety-nine percent sure Effie Tate was the kidnapper he'd been sent to track down. The question was, how could he remain true to his client without hurting Becky, not to mention sort out this muddle the way poor old Fred wanted?

Logan crossed the room in pursuit of Becky, politely returning the nods of acknowledgement he was getting as he passed. Chances were, everyone knew who he was—or rather, who he was supposed to be. He imagined, when all this was over, the good citizens of Serenity would be ready to run him out of town on a rail.

He snorted derisively. If that was all they did, he'd count himself lucky. He just hoped they were short on tar and feathers when the time came.

Effie confronted Becky as soon as she walked in the door that evening. "I heard where you were today, missy."

"I'm sure you did. I was hoping Brother Fred would call and tell you it was his idea, not mine. I couldn't very well turn him down when he asked me to show Logan around town."

"I'll have to have a talk with that Fred all right," Effie grumbled. "He ought to know better'n to send a pretty young thing like you out with the likes of that new preacher. I don't trust him as far as I could throw him."

"None of us are looking forward to change," Becky said gently. "But we all know Fred deserves his retirement. And Brother Logan isn't permanent. While he's here, you really should treat him with the respect due his calling."

"Bah. Respect, my eye. There's somethin' shifty about that man. Mark my words, he's hidin' something."

How could she admit to thinking the same thing without making Effie's delusional condition worse? "I guess he had a bad time while he was in the army.

He doesn't like to talk about it. I hear lots of folks have trouble adjusting to civilian life again after they get out of the service."

"Well, well." The elderly woman plopped down on the settee, grinned at Becky, and gave a noisy, theatrical wheeze. "Tell Fred my asthma's kickin' up again and I'd like for him to stop by."

"You know that's not fair. Fred has other folks to minister to. Ones who are really sick. He only has so much time to give each day. If you monopolize him, somebody else may have to go without."

She began to smile as an idea took shape. "Tell you what. How about I send Brother Logan over, instead? Then you and he can get to know each other."

"No!" It was a shout.

"Why not?"

Seeing the dread in her aunt's expression, the sudden stiffness of her body, Becky realized she'd momentarily dropped her guard and forgotten to choose her words carefully enough.

Seeking to make amends, she joined Effie on the sofa and put her arm around the elderly woman's thin shoulders. "Never mind. I'll tell Fred, just like you wanted. And I won't ask Brother Logan to come by. I promise."

"You're a good girl," Effie whispered.

"I try." The sentimental compliment nearly brought tears to Becky's eyes.

"We won't let 'em get us."

"That's right," Becky agreed sadly. "You and I will stick together no matter what."

As she gently rocked her aunt to soothe her, she reinforced that vow in her heart. Effie had cared for her when she was a helpless baby. Now that the tables were turned, it was Becky's duty to become the acting parent. The source of strength and wisdom. The decision maker.

It wasn't a position she'd sought. Nor was it one she felt comfortable with. It was simply a necessity. Something she must do.

She was positive the Lord wouldn't give her a task she couldn't cope with, but at times like this, she wished He didn't think quite so highly of her capabilities.

Logan had stopped at the local market to pick up a few things for Fred and was headed home. He flipped open his cell phone as he drove and punched a prerecorded number. An answering machine picked up the call.

"This is Logan Malloy," he said, giving the date and time for reference. "Sandra, type this report and fax it to Mr. Dan Keringhoven. The number's in the file. You'll know how to word it. Tell him I'm on the job. I've made some contacts and things are progressing as expected. However, I don't have anything definitive for him yet."

He paused, hoping lightning wasn't going to strike him if he stretched the truth a bit more. "I advise we take our time with this investigation if we want to get everything sorted out to his satisfaction. Be sure he understands that. Tell him I'll phone him as soon as I have positive proof, one way or the other. Thanks."

Logan ended the call as he pulled into Fred's driveway. He found his friend pacing the room he used as his home office and paused in the doorway with the sacks of groceries. "I got most of the stuff you wanted. The chicken was about to go out of date so I bought steaks. My treat. Hope that's okay."

"Sounds great. So, did you find out anything useful today?"

"Not much. Let's go put this stuff away before it spoils." He led the way to the kitchen.

Fred followed. "At least tell me what you think."

"Okay," Logan said with a sigh. "I think I'll be stuck until I have a chance to talk to the aunt. How long has she been mentally unbalanced?"

"I wouldn't go that far," Fred argued. "Effie's had a rough life. I have trouble believing she's as ill as you seem to think she is."

"Tell me more about her." He opened the refrigerator and put the meat away. "Were you living here when she moved to town?"

"Yes. Part of the time. I was attending college over in Walnut Ridge but I came home every chance I got. Serenity Chapel didn't even exist back then." He signed and shook his head. "Effie Tate showed up here during my summer vacation. She was the prettiest girl I'd ever seen."

That statement got Logan's full attention. "Whoa. What about Gracie?"

"I wasn't married to her then," Fred said. "We hadn't even met. If Effie would have had me, she and I could have raised that baby of hers together. But she wasn't ready for a husband. When I went back to school, I fell in love with Gracie. End of story."

"Not hardly. Do you think Effie had feelings for you?"

"I suppose she might have. She never admitted anything. After I was married, we never spoke of it again."

"But you're friends, aren't you?"

"As much as is appropriate. I've never done anything that would dishonor my calling." He stared at Logan. "And I never will, so don't even ask."

"Hey, don't get defensive. I'm not suggesting you step out of line. But you are a widower. Doesn't it seem natural that you might want companionship in your old age?"

"If I get lonesome I'll get a dog."

Logan laughed. "You don't fool me. There's still a warm spot in your heart for Effie Tate. Admit it."

"I've never denied it. That's why I refuse to help you send her to prison. Don't make me sorry I confided in you and let you come here."

"You're already assuming she's guilty, aren't you?"

Fred's nostrils flared in anger. "I never said that. You're twisting everything. Effie's one of the most loving people I've ever had the privilege to know. I won't be a party to anything that might hurt her."

"Then why did you tell me the truth?" Logan made a face. "Never mind. I know the answer. And I respect you for your honesty. But you're forgetting the purpose of my investigation. A baby was kidnapped. It doesn't matter how long ago the abduction occurred, it's still a crime."

"I know."

Logan was sorry to see the old man's shoulders slump when he made that admission. "Look, Fred," he said, giving his mentor an encouraging pat on the back, "I don't want to see you hurt, either. Don't worry about a thing. I'll handle the girl and her aunt by myself."

"Oh, really?" Fred apparently set his concern aside enough to manage a lopsided smile. "That should be interesting. How do you plan to proceed?"

"I'll get into Becky's good graces and ask her to help me deal with her aunt. It shouldn't take too long." He was surprised to hear the older man chuckle. "What's so funny?"

"Nothing. Just thinking," Fred said. "I'm glad I haven't retired yet. I'm looking forward to seeing you try to manipulate those two stubborn, intelligent women. It should be real entertaining."

Chapter Six

Becky looked forward to Sunday mornings, especially since she'd joined Miss Louella's Extraordinary Ladies class. It was the most popular and the most aptly named group at Serenity Chapel. Becky wasn't certain when the word *Extraordinary* had been added to the description. She simply knew that was where she belonged. And she didn't mind one bit that she was younger than most of the other women who attended regularly.

Walking into that classroom always gave Becky the feeling of a happy family reunion. This morning was no exception. There were usually plenty of aches and pains mentioned, as well as prayer requests for others, yet the welcome aura of peace and love easily overshadowed the negative.

Miss Louella Higgen's smile was as broad as the rest of her when she greeted Becky with a hug and a welcoming, "Glad to see you," followed by a wink and a query. "So, what's new? I notice you've got your best dress on."

Becky ignored the background chuckles. She shrugged. "Not much. I happen to like this dress."

The class's reaction was unanimous disbelief, expressed in several subdued but evident ways, including whispers and snickers.

Miss Louella rapped on the podium. "Now, now. It's none of our business if Becky wants to go cavorting all over town with a handsome stranger and get all those tongues to wagging. We'll love her even if she backslides, won't we? Of course we will." She suppressed a titter of her own. "Maybe we'd best just pray for her real hard and leave the rest to the Good Lord."

Becky blew a loud sigh. "Oh, for crying out loud…." She sank into her usual seat at the end of the second row of folding chairs. "It's no secret. I took Brother Malloy on a short tour around town. We stopped at the chamber and then had lunch at Bea's. Anything else y'all want to know?"

The questions came at her in a rush. She chose to answer the easiest few. "Yes, he's nice. And polite. He has wonderful manners. But Brother Fred is right about his not fitting in here very well. I don't think Logan is the preacher for us. I'm sure he'll make a fine substitute until we can find Fred's replacement, though."

She waved her hands to request quiet. "Simmer down. I don't know much more about the man than you all do. He's not real talkative."

"All right. Hush." Louella called for order. "Looks like we'd best add finding a new preacher to our list of prayer requests. Anybody else? How's your aunt doing, Becky?"

"She has her ups and downs. Change seems to really bother her. She's having a hard time adjusting to Brother Logan being here, even temporarily. I suppose that's natural. No matter who we choose, we'll always miss Fred."

There was a chorus of agreement.

"I wanted to bring in that young fella from over by Jonesboro and let him show us what he can do," widowed Carol Sue Grabowski announced from the back of the room. "Don't see what's takin' the pulpit committee so long to make a move. You'd think Brother Fred didn't want to let go."

"I suppose he doesn't," Becky said. She pivoted to face everyone. "He doesn't realize it, of course. He's really going to be at loose ends when he doesn't have a job to go to every day."

"Or anybody to come home to," Miss Louella said. "I figured one of us single ladies would've snagged him by now. There's plenty to choose from right here in this room."

"Louella!" Carol Sue blurted, her cheeks reddening. Others merely laughed softly or mumbled.

"Well, I did," the teacher said. "If you can't speak the truth in the Lord's house, where can you speak it?"

"That's very true," Becky agreed. "I'd like to see him find a nice lady to share his old age, too."

"What about Effie?" Mercy Cosgrove piped up. "Seems to me they need each other. Fred used to be sweet on her. Maybe he still is?"

That revelation took Rebecca by complete surprise. "He did? They were? I mean, Fred and Effie were a couple? That's amazing." No wonder Effie had always run to Fred for advice when she'd had problems she couldn't solve alone. All this time, Becky had assumed Effie was simply relying on their pastor the way everyone else did. Hearing that they might share a deeper friendship was quite a shock.

Continuing to grin like a cat with bird feathers clinging to its whiskers, Mercy nodded. "Yup. I remember it well. You was just a tiny thing back then. Hardly more'n a couple of months old. Fred cut a dashing figure in those days. Every bit as handsome as that Logan Malloy. All the girls wanted to marry him. All except Effie. She got on her high horse about it and poor Fred went off and found him a wife somewhere else."

"Gracie Fleming was a lovely woman. Perfect for Brother Fred," Becky insisted.

"Sure she was. But she's been gone for two years now. Why do you suppose Fred hasn't looked around more? Enough of us have asked him over to Sunday dinner and filled him up with our fried chicken and homemade pies. I think he's still stuck on Effie, more's the pity."

Rebecca took a deep breath and released it as a slow sigh. If that was the case, he'd probably waited too long. Effie's mental state was less than conducive to a happily-ever-after scenario. Still, the Lord did move in mysterious ways sometimes.

"Brother Logan mentioned a new medicine that might help my aunt," Becky said. "I'm going to ask Dr. Sam about it."

"Good." Louella was making notes, as were most of the others. "Now that that's settled, who else has a prayer request or a praise to share? Time's a wastin'."

Logan was hanging back near the sanctuary door, helping Brother Fred greet parishioners who hadn't attended Sunday school. He'd seen Becky breeze into her classroom an hour earlier but he hadn't spotted Effie Tate yet. Hopefully, she'd pass by and give Fred the chance to introduce him on neutral ground. Effie was far less likely to spit in his eye or turn and run if she felt safely surrounded by friends.

Scanning the parking lot, Logan saw the church minibus arrive and begin to disgorge its passengers. His quarry was among them. He elbowed Fred and stepped back. "Here she comes. Ready?"

The older man nodded and reached for Effie's hand, grasping it firmly before he said, "Effie, dear, I'd like to introduce Brother Logan Malloy. You remember him, don't you? He helped you and Rebecca get down off the roof."

Squinting past Fred's shoulder, Effie glared. "I remember him all right. He liked to scare me to death."

"He's an old friend of mine," Fred continued. "A good friend." He stood to one side and passed her hand to Logan as if they were exchanging a precious, fragile commodity.

Logan felt her tremble when he accepted her hand but she stood her ground. He smiled. "Pleased to meet you, ma'am. I wish you and I had gotten off to a better start."

Staring up at him, Effie said clearly, "It's not the

beginning that concerns me, young man. It's how everything ends."

He assumed she was referring to spiritual matters. "I'm sure heaven is a wonderful place."

"Heaven?" The elderly eyes narrowed. "Ha! I'm not near ready to take that trip yet. Got too many things to take care of down here."

"Don't we all. I'm staying with Brother Fred while I'm in town. If you ever need my help or want to talk, feel free to call. Day or night. That's what I'm here for."

Eyebrows arching, she pulled her hand away. "Is it? We'll see."

Watching her walk off, Logan was puzzled. If that woman was senile, she was giving an awfully good impression of cleverness and dry wit. He supposed it was possible she'd been confused and he'd misconstrued her comments as being cunning, but he doubted it. He'd stake his reputation that there was a lot more to Effie Tate than most people suspected. He just hoped he could find out the whole truth and bring this investigation to a suitable conclusion before his employer got impatient and interfered, the way he'd threatened to.

Mr. Keringhoven did deserve to hear that he'd made a little progress, which he had, but he wasn't ready to reveal any details. Not yet. His solemn promise to Fred Fleming took precedence over everything else, even his job. No one was going to storm into town and destroy the Tate family because of supposition. Justice had waited this long. It could wait a little longer. Eventually the real truth would come out.

Rebecca's usual place was in the center of the front row where she could more easily distribute and collect the information cards that prospective members filled out. Consequently, she faced the pulpit. Beside it, to the left, sat Dub Robinson, the gray-haired choir director. Logan sat on the other side. He was wearing a dark suit this morning, and the same kind of plain shirt and tie Brother Fleming favored. That was where their similarity ended. Logan seemed larger than life and twice as handsome.

Her cheeks warmed. Becky looked away, grateful that her back was to the ladies from her Sunday school class. The last thing she needed was to have them see her blush because of Logan.

His eyes met hers. He smiled slightly.

Becky nodded a friendly response, then busied herself with the membership folder she always brought to the service. Anything but continue to look at him, although she didn't have a clue how she was going to listen to Fred's sermon without glancing past him and seeing Logan. The more she tried to avoid doing so, the more her attention drifted in that direction.

She was so intent on *not* looking, she didn't notice she had company until she heard, "Scoot over, girl."

Becky was startled. "Aunt Effie? What brings you down front? I thought you liked to be by the door in the back?"

"Still do. Just don't want you sittin' up here all alone."

Rebecca grinned at the rapidly filling pew as she tucked her skirt closer to make room. "I'm hardly alone, Aunt Effie. But you're more than welcome to join me. I like it in the front. There aren't as many distractions."

"Humph. 'Cept the fellas up there," the older woman said with lifted eyebrows. "Leastwise we can keep track of 'em from here."

"That's true." Becky pulled a face. "And they can watch us. When I was a teenager I used to think Brother Fred was preaching straight to me. It really made me nervous." She laughed quietly. "Especially if I was chewing gum or doing something else I thought he wouldn't like."

Effie snorted. "Why do you think I always sit near the back? That Fred can really get to me when he goes to preachin' serious."

Leaning closer to speak in confidence, Becky said, "I'm looking forward to hearing how Brother Logan does when he finally takes a turn at it. I don't think he's too thrilled with the idea of giving a sermon."

"Don't you think that's a bit strange?"

"Yes and no," Becky answered. "He's from the city. I suspect he knows he's going to have trouble getting this congregation to relate to him."

"Maybe." Effie sat straighter and carefully smoothed her dark navy skirt over her knees. "Or maybe he's afraid everybody'll see right through him."

Before Becky could comment, the elderly woman glared at him and added, "I sure do."

"Aunt Effie!"

"Well, I do. You would, too, if you wasn't so young and foolish. Flo was like that, too. Walked right into the devil's pretty trap with her eyes wide open."

"Who, exactly, is…?"

Before Becky could form the rest of her query, the organist cranked up the volume and the choir began to file in, singing. Resigned, Becky sat back. She'd missed another perfect chance to question Effie. Oh, well, there was bound to be another. This was the first time in recent memory her aunt had spoken of

Flo without sounding confused. That was not only a good sign, it gave Becky hope that she'd soon get an opportunity to ask for more specifics.

Though she stood with the congregation to sing the first hymn, her mind was still puzzling. There had to be a reason why memories of Florence had suddenly begun crowding her aunt's thoughts, why the elderly woman often mistook her for whoever Flo was.

Perhaps if she could convince Effie to talk about the past and identify the personal demons that had started haunting her so vividly, her mental state would improve.

This wasn't the first time that notion had occurred to Becky. Was God answering her prayers by suggesting the underlying reason for poor Effie's turmoil? That seemed almost too simple, too pat. Yet there were cases on record where guilt had eroded sanity enough to cause symptoms of illness.

Rebecca raised her gaze to Brother Fred and found him looking at her with an expression of tender concern. She smiled at him.

Instead of returning the amiable gesture, he shifted his awareness to Effie and began blinking rapidly. When he took out his handkerchief and blew his nose, Becky had to resist the urge to jump out of her seat and rush forward to give him a comforting hug.

Something was really bothering Fred. And he wasn't the only one. Beside her, Aunt Effie had begun to sniffle, too.

Becky looked back and forth, alternating between the two people she loved most in the whole world. Whatever was wrong, she was going to find out and then fix it, even if that meant she had to use the information she'd garnered in class and play matchmaker for the most unlikely couple she'd ever known.

Chapter Seven

Becky prayed Brother Fred through his sermon, asking the Lord to sustain him and give him the strength to carry on as usual. His struggle became hers. Though the congregation was dismissed a few minutes before noon, the service still felt like the longest one she'd ever sat through.

Gathering up her Bible and the membership file, she stood and waited for Effie. The older woman acted glued to the padded pew. "I need to drop this folder in the office," Becky said. "Want to keep me company?"

"Sure." Effie stood slowly, stiffly. "I want to hang around anyway and talk to Fred before I go. I'm in no hurry to tangle with that new preacher, though. Not again."

"You talked to Brother Logan? When?"

"This morning."

"You didn't give him trouble, did you?"

"No more than he deserved," Effie said flatly. "I was thinkin' of askin' Fred to come to Sunday dinner today. That okay with you?"

"It's fine. More than fine," Becky said. "He seemed a little out-of-sorts this morning. Probably needs a good dose of your home cooking." *And having Fred there for moral support will give me the perfect chance to ask questions without you getting as upset as usual.*

"Good." Effie seemed to miraculously gain energy. "You get that Logan fella away from our Fred so's I can ask him."

"Don't you think it's impolite to exclude Brother Malloy? I mean, he is staying at Fred's. And they are old friends."

"I don't want that man in my house."

"Why not?"

"I've got my reasons."

"I know. You've told me often enough how you feel about most men. Don't you think we should make an exception in Brother Logan's case? For Fred's sake, I mean."

Effie scrunched up her face. "Humph. Seems to me this whole idea's gotten out of hand. Let's forget it."

"No, no. It'll do us good to have company. And I know the visit will be good for Fred. Let me handle it. We do have enough to feed four, don't we?"

"I put a whole roast in the Crock-Pot. I 'spect it'll do if we mash some extra taters and make gravy. But…"

"All right." Becky worked at acting eager. "Then it's settled. Do you want to ride the bus home or shall I pick you up after I talk to Brother Fred?"

"What're you askin' *me* for? What I want doesn't seem to matter much anymore."

"Of course it does." She patted Effie's hand. "You know as well as I do that excluding Brother Malloy is unkind. You can be a little stubborn sometimes, we all can, but you're not mean-spirited."

Effie's expression showed disgust, followed by reluctant capitulation. "Okay. Do it your way. I'll go home and get busy. Don't hurry on my account. You can set the table when you get there."

"Fine."

She waited for her aunt to start for the side door where the church bus always waited. Instead, the older woman stood motionless, staring into space. "The bus is that way," Becky finally said, pointing.

Effie's head snapped around. "I know."

Watching her amble off, Becky wondered if she had known which way to go or if she was simply covering another mental lapse. Either was possible. If Effie was really that ill, was it fair to Fred to encourage him to renew their courtship?

That question brought a smile. *Why not?* It wasn't up to her to decide the outcome. And if two people were ever suited for each other, it was Brother Fred and Aunt Effie. Talk about two peas in a pod!

Sweet peas, she added, grinning. *Definitely sweet peas.*

Becky stood aside in the foyer, waiting patiently until Brother Fred and Brother Logan had bid each departing member of the congregation a pleasant goodbye.

As they closed the door, she heard Logan ask the older man, "You okay?" and saw an answering nod.

It was Fred she approached. "Nice sermon."

"Thanks." He blotted his brow. "I think the air-conditioning needs adjusting again. Remind me to ask the custodian to see to it tomorrow."

"Okay."

Logan had stepped so close Becky was having trouble concentrating on her boss. "Uh, Aunt Effie wanted me to invite you to dinner." She gave a nervous little cough. "Both of you."

"Well…" Fred's eyes narrowed.

Smiling, Logan patted him on the back. "We'd

love to come. Mind if I run home and ditch this tie first?"

Becky tried not to show how surprised she was that the easy acceptance had come from Logan rather than her beloved employer. "No problem. We'll eat between one-thirty and two. Will that give you enough time?"

All she got from Brother Fred was a nod. It was Logan who said, "Sounds perfect. Can we bring anything?"

"No. Aunt Effie has a roast already cooked. I'm sure we have plenty of food. Thanks for asking." She backpedaled. "Well, I'd better head home to help."

"Don't go to any trouble," Logan said. "We want you to treat us just like you would family. Don't we, Fred?"

The older man gave Becky a slow, tender smile, his eyes once again beginning to glisten. "We are family. If Gracie and I had been blessed with children, I couldn't love them any more than I do Rebecca."

This time, she was close enough to give him a comforting hug without displaying it in front of the whole congregation. No explanation was necessary. She simply stepped up to Brother Fred and put her arms around him.

"I love you, too," she said, getting misty-eyed herself. "I wish you *were* my real dad."

All he said was, "So do I."

* * *

Logan drove Fred home. He waited until they were inside the white, two-storey house on Squirrel Hill Road before he said, "You're *not* Becky's father, you know."

The older man's head snapped around. "You don't have to remind me."

"I think maybe I do." Logan dropped his jacket on a chair, then pulled off his tie and unbuttoned the neck and cuffs of his dress shirt. "Try to put yourself in that guy's place. How would you feel?"

Instead of answering, Fred said, "Never mind how I'd feel. Seems to me you've been assuming too much. How can you be so sure of your client's motives? Suppose it's revenge he wants? And suppose Effie isn't guilty? What if you throw her to the wolves and later discover you're wrong. What then?"

"I'm not throwing anybody to the wolves. My client is only interested in justice."

"I don't want a character reference. I want to know what you intend to do if you realize too late that the man is vindictive."

Fred's query was too perceptive to sit well with Logan. It wasn't his job to judge a client's heart. All he was hired to do was locate missing persons, report his findings, and leave the rest to law enforcement. It had already occurred to him that this job was a special case, particularly when he'd learned that his quarry might be living in the same town his old friend called home.

At first, that news had seemed providential; a walk in the park. Now, however, he was beginning to wonder if this pursuit was going to be more like blundering into quicksand, instead. There wasn't anyone left who meant more to him than Fred Fleming. And apparently, there weren't many people as dear to Fred as Becky and her aunt.

Logan knew he couldn't just walk away, no matter how much he wanted to. If he tried to abdicate his duty, his client would simply send someone else and keep searching Serenity and its environs until he was satisfied.

Ethics—and conscience—precluded Logan's lying. He was, however, open to using delaying tactics when necessary. That was why he'd called in such an ambiguous report.

While Fred was in the bedroom changing into casual clothes, Logan phoned his office to check for messages. He was concluding his business when Fred returned and took up their conversation where it had left off.

"You don't have a shred of real proof," the older man said.

"I know. And I won't act on unfounded suspicions. But I am looking forward to having dinner with the prime suspect."

Muttering, Fred hitched up his slacks. "Then go get changed or whatever you're going to do and let's make tracks. The sooner we get this over with and you see you're barking up the wrong tree, the better I'll feel."

"Barking?" Logan laughed.

"Yeah. I used to have a dumb old hound that acted just like you. He'd get it into his thick head that a squirrel was in a certain tree because he'd seen him run up it. No matter how hard I tried, I couldn't convince that dog the squirrel had jumped to another treetop and was long gone."

"Meaning?"

"Meaning, I'm no detective, but a few ideas have come to mind. One, your caller might have been passing through and just stopped in Serenity to use a pay phone. And two, if Becky wanted to call someone, why wouldn't she use her cell phone? One mysterious telephone call seems like an awfully thin clue to base a whole investigation on."

"It is," Logan said. "But even a hound dog has to start by sniffing around before he can decide which way to go. That's all I'm doing."

Fred bristled. "You just mind where that sniffing leads. My cooperation ends the minute you do anything to upset Effie."

"Even if she's guilty?" Logan asked quietly.

The look of disdain Fred shot his way was all the answer he needed.

"I thought we weren't going to fuss?" Becky arched an eyebrow. "Looks to me like you've gone overboard."

"Nonsense. Brother Fred loves my fried pies." Effie expertly flipped the half-moon-shaped dough pocket bubbling in the skillet. "I made apple. It's his favorite."

"You and Fred have been friends for a long time." She hesitated a heartbeat. "Funny you two never got together. Romantically, I mean."

"The man was married."

"Not when you first met him."

Effie pointed with the spatula. "What do you know about that? Who's been blabbing?"

"Nobody special." Becky continued to lay the silverware beside the plates spaced at compass points around the circular table. "We were talking about it this morning in class. Somebody remembered that you and Fred had been pretty close, once. They said he even asked you to marry him. I wondered why you'd never mentioned it. You didn't turn him down because of me, did you?"

The older woman blanched in spite of the heat

from the frying pan. "'Course not. I've told you how I feel plenty of times. Fred's the sweetest man I know but he's still a man. None of 'em can be trusted. 'Specially not…"

"Especially not who?"

"Never mind. I'm a silly old fool, that's all. You got the table set?"

Rebecca squinted at her across the farm-style kitchen. "The table's fine. But you're not. It's high time you told me exactly why you're so dead set against men—particularly good-looking ones."

"Handsome is as handsome does. I got nothin' against 'em, long as they behave themselves."

"Brother Fred has always been polite and kind, to us as well as to everybody else. How can you lump him in with all the others?"

"Self-preservation," Effie said. "There's only one way for a woman to be sure she's safe and that's to take care of herself." She smiled at Becky, then sniffled and turned to tend the frying pan before she added, "Herself, and her innocent babies."

There had been instances, during Becky's childhood, when she'd pretended Effie was her birth mother. She'd never asked directly until now. "Are you my mother?"

"I've done my best to be."

"I know you have." Becky approached and patted her aunt's thin shoulder, taking care to keep them both out of range of splattering cooking oil. "No one could have done a better job of raising me. What I meant was, did you invent the story about my parents so I wouldn't be ashamed of not having a daddy?"

Effie's jaw dropped. "Sakes alive, no. What ever gave you that idea?"

"Partly the wild stories you used to tell when I was a kid. I was never sure whether they were true or whether you were making them up to entertain me." She chuckled. "I am pretty sure I'm not the granddaughter of a princess."

"Sometimes the truth is a lot harder to swallow than a good, made-up story."

"I'm not a kid anymore. I'm all grown up. I want to know the whole truth, Aunt Effie. Tell me? Please?"

The elderly woman sighed and shook her head. "Not right now. Let me chew on the idea for awhile. Could be the best thing I can do is keep my mouth shut, like I have been."

"That can't be right. The truth is supposed to set us free, remember?"

"*This* truth won't," Effie said flatly.

"How do you know? How can you be so sure?"

Tears glistened in the old woman's eyes. "Because, chances are, this truth got your mama killed."

Chapter Eight

After her aunt's astounding disclosure, it was all Becky could do to act seminormal, let alone carry on pleasant, dinner-table conversation. She not only wasn't sure she was making sense, she couldn't recall half of what had been said, other than, "Please pass the potatoes," or "Would you like gravy?" If she wasn't careful, folks would start imagining she was as dotty as her poor aunt. Right now, that was exactly how she felt.

Effie had clammed up completely after making the comment about Becky's late mother. Fred had arrived with Logan moments later, giving Becky no more private time with her aunt in which to probe for details.

Consequently, Becky was beside herself. The duration of the morning's sermon was nothing compared to the way the afternoon was dragging by. Time was creeping like a snail in January. A frozen snail. That image did nothing for her appetite.

Brother Fred didn't seem hungry, either. Though he'd always loved Effie's home cooking, he wasn't eating enough this time to keep Thelma McEntire's toy poodle happy. Which reminded her of an idea she'd been kicking around.

She voiced it. "I was thinking of getting a dog to keep Aunt Effie company. I was going to wait till Christmas to give it to her but maybe sooner is better."

The astonished expression on her aunt's face was so comical she had to laugh. "It can't be good for you to be home alone all day. Everybody needs companionship. Don't you think so, Brother Fred?"

Fred swallowed wrong and coughed into his napkin. "I, uh, I was just telling Logan the same thing. Dogs make wonderful companions. I used to keep hounds. Remember?"

"Of course, I do," Becky said brightly. "One was a great big black-and-tan dog called Homer. I used to sit on your porch and tell that dog all my troubles while Aunt Effie helped Gracie bake for church suppers. Homer had soft, floppy ears that felt like warm velvet."

"Dogs are nothin' but fleas and hair with an attitude," Effie piped up. "Never did see the use in 'em."

Finally, a subject that everyone could discuss even if their opinions did differ, Becky thought with relief. She glanced at Logan. "Did you have a dog when you were a little boy?"

"No." He shook his head. "But I have worked with a few."

"Really? What's your favorite breed?"

"We used German shepherds. They were great for foot patrols. Never missed a thing," he said flatly.

Oh, dear. He'd told her he'd been in the military and had indicated he didn't want to talk about those experiences. What should she say now? What could she say?

Fred came to the rescue. "Logan was an MP."

"Oh? Military police? How interesting."

No one else commented. Looking from Fred to Logan to Effie, Becky was struck by the difference in each one's expression. Fred seemed to be contemplating poignant thoughts and Effie was scowling like she wished she could boot Logan out the nearest door. When Becky looked at Logan he was staring back at her as if trying to delve into her subconscious and uncover secrets she didn't even know she had. Of all their reactions, his was by far the most unsettling. And the most compelling.

Her heart went out to him. "It must have been

very hard to reconcile your beliefs with such a dangerous assignment," she said softly.

A fleeting air of empathy and understanding connected them, giving Becky the shivers. Clearly, she'd touched on a point of conflict Logan didn't often acknowledge. She gave him a smile of encouragement. Instead of the amiable response she'd anticipated, however, he began to scowl.

"There is no way to reconcile my faith with taking a human life," he said. "The only way to deal with it is to close down your rational mind and rely on your reflexes for survival."

"It must feel really good to put all that behind you. I'm glad Brother Fred was able to offer you this chance to get back to preaching. How long have you been out of the army?"

Because she'd expected him to cite a recent date, it was a surprise to hear, "I was discharged five years ago."

"Really?"

Her gaze flashed an unspoken question to Fred. The shake of the older man's head was barely perceptible but his warning was clear. If she wanted to find out where Logan had been and what he'd been doing for the past five years, she needed to choose a better time to ask.

"So, let's get back to the subject of Aunt Effie's

Christmas puppy," she suggested. "What kind of a dog should I be looking for?"

"Invisible," the older woman grumbled. "The kind that never makes a mess or chews my shoes or leaves hair all over the house."

Becky chuckled. "Has anybody ever told you you're hard to please?"

"Mostly everybody," Effie said dryly. "But I've saved your bacon, missy. More than once."

Across the table, Fred twitched like he'd been poked with a pin. "Effie!"

"Well, I have," she insisted. "And I'll keep on doin' it as long as there's a spark of life in this old body."

The room stilled. It was as if they'd all stopped breathing. Effie was glaring at Logan. Fred was staring, openmouthed at Effie. And Logan had eased back in his chair as if waiting for further outbursts.

Becky could hear her own heart pounding. What had just happened? Could it be connected to Effie's comments about her mother's death? Waiting with the others, she imagined she saw uncommon apprehension in Brother Fred's eyes. If he was frightened, there had to be good reason. That conclusion alarmed her more than anything else.

Effie had broken the silence by jumping to her feet and announcing dessert. Logan watched her walk stiffly across the kitchen and return with a plate of pastry.

"Fried apple pies," she said, offering the plate to Fred. "Your favorite."

"They certainly are." He patted his ample stomach. "Wish I had room."

"You can take 'em with you if you want."

"Absolutely," Becky agreed. "I don't need all those extra calories." She included Logan, even though Effie wasn't even acknowledging his presence. "How about you, Brother Malloy? They're really good."

He was about to reach for one of the small half circles of puffy dough when his cell phone rang. He got to his feet. "I'll take this outside. Don't let me break up the party."

There was no chatter behind him to cover his pending conversation so he continued to his car, faced the street and leaned a hip against the fender. "This is Logan Malloy."

"I'm sorry, sir," the caller said. "I did as you asked and faxed that report to Mr. Keringhoven, but he's not a happy camper. He insists on speaking to you personally."

"That's okay, Sandra. Tell him I'll call him in a day or so."

"I'm afraid that won't do. He's really steamed."

The secretary lowered her voice. "He found out where I live and showed up here."

"At *your* place?"

"Yes. He says he's going to stay till I tell him how to reach you. I figured it was better to place the call myself than to give him your unlisted number."

"You did the right thing, Sandra. Put him on."

Logan didn't give the angry man a chance to say anything beyond, "Malloy?" before breaking in.

"Your behavior is way out of line, Keringhoven. My people take orders from me, not from our clients. I'll give you a full report when I'm ready and not before. Is that clear?"

"Very." The man on the other end of the line sounded gruff, hoarse.

"Good. Then we understand each other. I'll call you at your home number later today and tell you what little I've learned so far. Be there."

"In other words, get out of your secretary's hair?"

"Exactly. Sandra is my employee, not my confidante. She isn't hiding anything from you." His conscience twitched when he added, "Neither am I," though the claim was essentially true. He hadn't been able to prove Effie's story was false, nor had he been able to substantiate her claim of kinship to Rebecca. Without insisting on DNA evidence or getting the older woman to confess, he was stymied. Temporarily.

"Look," Logan said, "I think I'm getting close. The less I'm distracted by unnecessary interruptions like this, the better. Put Sandra back on."

He heard vague conversation in the background before his secretary returned.

"He's leaving," Sandra said, obviously relieved.

"Good. If he so much as looks at you funny again, I want to know. I'll stay on the line till you're sure he's long gone."

"He's driving away. I'm locking the door now," she said. "Do you think he'll come back?"

"He'd better not. When I talk to him tonight I'll warn him we'll drop his case if he doesn't behave himself."

"I thought you were worried about your old friend."

"I was. I am. I'm going to see this through whether it's an official job or not."

"Okay, boss. But I'm putting in a request for hazardous duty pay."

Logan laughed. "Do it. I'll tell Pete it's okay and have him write you a bonus check. Take care, kid."

Waiting till Sandra hung up, Logan folded the phone and slipped it back into his pocket. Part of him wished he'd never gotten involved in this investigation, while another part knew it had been inevitable. A man didn't turn his back on a true friend, no matter what the personal cost. Once he'd established the connection to Serenity, and to Fred Fleming, he'd been obliged by loyalty to accept the case.

That didn't make his job any easier. If Logan had been dealing with strangers he'd have simply forged ahead according to the usual formula. In this case, however, he intended to take his time and bend as many rules as necessary. It looked like convincing Keringhoven to be patient was going to be the trickiest part of his plan.

Logan heaved a sigh. It was time to head back into the house and see if he could learn anything else relevant.

He straightened, looked up, and stifled an exclamation of self-reproach. Becky was standing barely thirty feet away, quietly watching. This was the second time she'd caught him unawares. The second time she could have overheard too much for her own good. There wouldn't be a third.

She hadn't meant to get close enough to eavesdrop when she'd wandered outside. She'd only wanted to give Fred and Effie a little privacy. When she'd spotted Logan leaning against his car with the phone still pressed to his ear, she'd paused on the front porch and waited politely for him to finish talking.

What little she had heard had sounded a bit odd but not particularly interesting. It was his wary, almost devious expression when he turned and spotted her that made her uneasy.

In seconds, he'd recovered his nonchalant demeanor. The rapid change in him gave her goose bumps and tickled the hair at her nape. She felt like saying, "Will the *real* Logan Malloy please step forward?"

Instead, she waved and held up a plastic bag. "I saved you a couple of pies. Are you ready to eat them?"

His smile was as amiable as ever, yet Becky gave an imperceptible shiver as he approached.

"I'll try one," he said, gesturing at the porch swing. "Why don't we sit out here? The weather's too nice to spend the whole day indoors."

"As long as we keep our feet firmly on the ground that's fine with me. No more ladders, okay?" Her misgivings were rapidly dissolving under the influence of Logan's captivating smile.

"That reminds me. How are Effie's baby birds doing?"

"Fine. Looks like they've all fledged. As soon as I'm positive they're gone for good I'm going to have the chimney cleaned and a better cap installed."

"I could do that for you." Taking a bite of the pie,

Logan cupped his other hand beneath it to catch the warm juice. "Hey, this is really good."

"You sound surprised."

"I am, a little. I'd never heard of frying pie. It's kind of like a turnover."

"Only heavier," Becky added.

"That's the truth. I won't be hungry for a week. Aren't you having one?"

"Maybe later." She hesitated, thinking about his offer to bird-proof the chimney. "I hate to ask you to climb up on the roof again, even for a good cause, but since you're going to stay…"

"Stay? What gave you that idea?"

She glanced toward his car and immediately rued the slip.

Logan stiffened, stopped eating. "How much did you hear?"

"Nothing. Well, not much. I wasn't snooping. I may have heard you mention hanging around as long as necessary. I assumed you were talking about staying in Serenity until we found a replacement for Brother Fred."

"What else?"

"Nothing." She scowled. "Don't look at me like that."

"Like what?"

"Like you think I'm guilty of something."

"Are you?"

The hackles on her neck pricked again. "I don't understand what's gotten into you. One minute you're nice and the next you're accusing me of who-knows-what. Does Brother Fred know you have a split personality? Is that why he didn't recommend you for a permanent position?"

"I'm sure Fred is acting in the best interests of his congregation. You said yourself that I don't belong in a place like this."

"I wasn't being derogatory. I was just repeating something you'd said. I wouldn't purposely hurt your feelings."

"You didn't. I happen to agree with you."

"Then *what* is your problem?"

His eyes darkened. His gaze was so steady, so penetrating, she felt as if it reached all the way to her soul and read her innermost thoughts.

"*You* are," Logan said. "The Word was right. I've discovered for myself how impossible it is to serve two masters."

"You mean the verses that say you'll love the one and hate the other?"

Logan huffed. "Yeah. That's about the size of it."

Chapter Nine

Becky didn't know when she'd been so wrung out. Maybe never. When she'd gone back into the house to get Logan a glass of milk to wash down the fried pie, she'd come upon Brother Fred embracing Aunt Effie while the older woman cried on his shoulder. Literally. They had both regarded her with so much sadness she felt like a first-century martyr about to be fed to the lions.

As soon as their dinner guests had left, Becky began to probe. "Are you feeling better now?"

"Good enough."

"Well, I'm not. I want to know what got you so upset?"

"I wasn't upset. Whatever gave you that idea?"

Becky huffed. "Oh, I don't know. Maybe the fact you were crying all over Brother Fred."

"I was just commiserating."

"About what?" She wasn't ready to give up.

"About bein' between a rock and a hard place, mostly." Effie managed a tight smile. "I can sure enough identify with him about that."

"Because of me?"

"'Course not. What put that silly notion in your head?"

"You did," Becky said. "Don't you think it's about time you told me about my mother? And not the runaway princess story. The truth about how and why she died."

"I don't know it all."

"Then tell me what you do know. Please?" Becky took her aunt's thin hand and led her out onto the porch she'd so recently shared with Logan. Evening was fast approaching. "Would you like your sweater?"

"No. I'm warm enough."

"Then sit down with me and let's swing while we talk. It'll relax you."

"You aren't aimin' to drop this, are you?"

"No. But I won't rush you. Take your time." Still holding Effie's hand, Becky patted it gently. "It'll be okay. I have a right to know."

Tears glistened in the other woman's eyes. "That doesn't make it wise for me to tell you."

"But it makes it fitting. You won't be telling

tales out of school. My parents are both dead, right?"

A tear crested and slid down Effie's cheek before she spoke. "Your mama and I were close. Real close. She was beautiful, just like you, but she wasn't grounded good. She was flighty. Got herself into a terrible mess."

"Is that what you meant by saying she fell for the devil's ways?"

"Sort of. The trouble started when she married your daddy. He seemed like a nice enough fella. I didn't dream he'd turn mean like he did."

Becky's fingers tightened on her aunt's.

Effie returned the squeeze. "You sure you want me to keep on?"

"Yes. Please."

"Well, things just got worse and worse between 'em. Pretty soon Flo was making excuses for supposed accidents and showing up with bruises."

"Whoa," Becky said, "you told me my mother's name was Rebecca, like mine."

"I lied. I had to. It was for your own good." Effie lowered her voice, stared without seeing, and spoke as if narrating a dream. "Flo had that sunshine hair like yours and the bluest eyes you ever saw. It broke my heart to see her gettin' hurt over and over again."

Becky's stomach was churning, her pulse racing. "My *father* did that to her?"

"Yes." Malice filled Effie's gaze.

"Are you positive?"

"Oh, yes. It wasn't too bad at first but after you came along, Flo and me decided to run away. We had it all planned." Effie sniffled and blinked back tears. "I was supposed to take you and meet her at a motel we'd picked out. Only she never showed up. By that time, she was dead."

Becky was so astounded she could hardly speak, let alone think straight. "And you *kept* me?"

"I had to. I couldn't send you back to him. Not after the way he'd treated your mama."

Becky's breath caught, her temples began to throb, her thoughts spun. "Wait a minute. Are you saying my father isn't dead?"

"I don't know what became of him. I don't want to know. That man was as evil as they come."

"But surely he looked for me. He must have." She got to her feet and began pacing the length of the wooden porch. "How did you manage to hide all these years? It can't be easy to just drop out of sight."

"It wasn't. I pulled a lot of shenanigans to keep you safe and sound."

The portent of Effie's confession was beginning

to sink in. The person she loved and admired most in the whole world was a fugitive. Unbelievable!

Effie had begun to weep in earnest. Tearful herself, Becky returned to the porch swing, put her arms around the old woman's thin shoulders and pulled her close.

Rocking back and forth, she ached with the anguish of the truth that had been kept from her for so long. All she said was, "Oh, Aunt Effie. What have you done? What have you done?"

The focus of the elderly eyes blurred as present reality faded. "I brought your baby, Flo, just like we'd planned," she said, wiping away the remnants of her tears and looking at Rebecca. "I been waitin' a long time. A real long time. I was beginnin' to think you wasn't comin.' Now you're here, we can get on with our business."

Becky's hold tightened with affection and she began to croon like a mother comforting a distressed child. "Of course we can. You don't have to worry anymore. I'll look after you. I promise. Everything will be fine."

Becky's thoughts were tumbling, refusing to rest. *Florence was my mother's name. But Florence what?* Probably not Tate, especially since she and her aunt currently shared the same last name. No telling where Effie had come up with that alias. Why she'd chosen to fabricate their past, however, was evident.

The most important question remaining was what would happen to poor Effie if the truth came out. Was there a statute of limitations? Becky doubted it. Even if the police were no longer involved, she'd still committed a crime. Reasons or no reasons, valid or not, what Effie had done was terribly wrong.

Going to her room, Becky opened the top drawer of her dresser, dug under her socks and retrieved the old family snapshot. In all the confusion, she'd forgotten about it. Now, the picture made perfect sense—except for the little boy. If she was the baby in Florence's arms, then who was the other child? And what had happened to him?

Asking Effie was out of the question for now. She hadn't been making much sense since her declaration of guilt and Becky didn't want to push her any farther.

She considered taking the picture to Brother Fred. All that was stopping her was Logan's continued involvement in Fred's daily life. Her hands began to tremble.

Logan.

He had arrived shortly after her aborted call to one of the Keringhoven numbers on her list. Was that an innocent coincidence?

It had to be, she reasoned. Logan and Fred were old friends. It was highly unlikely the two events were connected. Still, if she went to Fred with what she'd learned, might he tell Logan? Something told her she shouldn't take that chance.

Becky sank onto the edge of her bed, the photo clutched in her hands. If she were smart, she'd never talk to anybody about this. Ever. The responsibility Effie had been shouldering alone for over twenty-five years weighed so heavily on her she wondered how the poor woman had survived, let alone persevered and brought up a child by herself.

Rising, Becky returned the photo to the bottom of the drawer. Time was on their side. Since they hadn't been found yet, chances were they never would be. Unless…

Picturing Logan, she closed her eyes and sighed. There must be a clue she was missing; a sensible reason why Brother Fred had asked Logan to come to Serenity when so many other qualified men were already vying for the job.

The only result of her troubling thoughts was a twisting in her stomach and a sick feeling that stayed with her the rest of the day.

Going to work Monday morning was one of the hardest things Becky had ever made herself do. Facing Brother Fred wasn't easy, either. The look on his face as he wished her, "Good morning," was anything but *good*.

"Morning," she replied. "Where's Brother Malloy?"

"Um, outside, I guess."

"Probably making another mysterious call," Becky grumbled. "That man does love his little cell phone."

"He mentioned that you'd overheard him. Is there anything you'd like to share with me?"

"Like what?" The hair on her neck tingled. "Don't you trust him, either?"

Fred blinked rapidly and cleared his throat. "What do you mean, *either?* Are you having a problem with him?"

"No, but Aunt Effie sure is. That shouldn't be a surprise to you, seeing as she was crying on your shoulder yesterday. How much did she tell you?"

Clearly nervous, he ran his index finger under the front of his shirt collar as if it were choking him. "About what?"

Becky crossed the room, grasped his arm and pulled him with her into his private office. She shut the door and whirled to face him before she said, "About *me.*"

"I don't know what you mean."

If he hadn't seemed so ill-at-ease she might have

been tempted to believe his denial. "I think you do." Her voice gentled. "Look, Brother Fred, I'm more worried than angry. I don't want anything bad to happen to Aunt Effie. I love her dearly. I just don't know what to do."

"Nothing," Fred said flatly. "Do nothing." He cast a brief glance over his shoulder at the closed door and lowered his voice. "The best thing you and I can do is nothing at all."

"The committee for next year's Fulton County Homecoming will meet in our church basement to-night." Brother Fred was all business. Becky was taking notes while Logan perched nonchalantly on the edge of his desk and nodded.

"I won't be able to attend, so I've asked Brother Logan to go in my place. You'll be there, of course, Rebecca."

"Of course." The muscles in her neck and shoul-ders knotted, making her wish she'd followed her in-clination to call in sick that morning. *Keep up the tension like this and before long she really would be ill.*

"Good." Fred rose from behind his desk. "Well, I have hospital visits to make. One's all the way over in Mountain Home so don't expect me back in the office today."

"What about supper?" Logan asked. "Shall I fix enough for two?"

"No. I'll pick up something if I get hungry." He gave Becky a kindly smile and touched her hand. "Don't you worry about a thing. The Lord can handle any problem, no matter what it is, if we let Him."

The love and concern emanating from Fred warmed her heart and gave her some peace. "Thanks for reminding me."

"That's my job," he said with a wink. "You two behave yourselves while I'm gone, you hear."

"Brother Fred!" Becky was frowning. "You're starting to sound like the women in my Sunday school class."

Logan chuckled. "Trouble in paradise?"

"Nothing I can't handle, thank you." Following Fred to the outer door she asked, "Mind if I go home a little early? Brother Logan's going to be here. There's no sense in both of us sitting around waiting for the phone to ring, is there?"

"Fine with me," the older man said. He leaned closer and cupped his hand to add, "Don't worry about Effie. I'm taking her with me. The hospital chaplain has contacted a specialist who's agreed to meet us there and speak with her. Unofficially, of course."

Becky was overcome with gratitude. "Oh,

Brother Fred." She hugged his neck and kissed his cheek. "I love you."

Behind them, Logan was just stepping into the hallway. He cleared his throat. "Hey, what did I miss?"

"Nothing. Not a thing," she said, waving as Fred walked the final few feet to his car. "I was just reminding Brother Fred what a special pastor he is."

"I know that, and you know that, and Fred knows that," Logan drawled. "My only concern would be what somebody else might think if they saw you acting that way."

"Fred Fleming is like a father to me," she insisted. "And around here, folks are always showing affection. But you are right in a way. It isn't wise for you and me to stay here by ourselves. People might talk."

"More than usual, you mean?"

"Yes." She bustled back to her desk, pulled open the bottom drawer and retrieved her shoulder bag. "Fred gave me permission to go home early and I'm going to take him up on the offer." She pointed. "The answering machine is already on and there are plenty of blank message slips right here. They're the pink ones. The blue paper is for hospital notifications. If anybody calls to tell us about one of those, jot a note for Fred and leave it in the middle of my desk. I'll enter it into the computer and print a fresh list in the morning. Remember to lock up when you leave."

Logan saluted. "Yes, ma'am." He gave her a lop-sided grin. "Anything else? Scrub the floors, wash the windows, take out the trash, sweep the parking lot?"

She paused with her hand on the doorknob. "There is one other thing I've been meaning to mention. We're all allowed to make personal calls on the office phone. If you use it, jot down the number, date and time and I'll figure out what you owe when the bill comes."

"Is that what you do?" His smile faded.

"Sometimes. Sometimes I use my cell phone."

"Never a pay phone?"

The question took Becky's breath away. She prayed he couldn't tell she was being evasive when she stood tall and answered, "Don't be silly." The only time she'd used a public phone in past memory had been when she'd foolishly called a perfect stranger to ask about the old photo. Why in the world would Logan bring up using pay phones? The coincidence was more than unsettling. It was scary.

Chapter Ten

Effie still wasn't home by the time Becky had to return to unlock the church for the homecoming committee meeting. She wasn't usually this high-strung but in view of all that had happened in the past few days she supposed it was natural for her hands to tremble slightly when she inserted her key in the lock on the side door.

It wouldn't turn properly. Frowning, she tried again and found she was able to *lock* the door just fine. Logan had apparently neglected to follow her orders and secure the building when he'd left.

Mumbling to herself, she pushed open the heavy door and let it swing closed behind her on its own. The clang and clatter of the latch mechanism echoed down the deserted hallway and drowned out her footsteps.

She flipped on the basement lights and started down the carpeted stairs. It was a journey she'd made countless times. Although she was used to being the first one there and the last one to leave, and to working alone in the cavernous building, this was the first time she'd noticed how quiet the place was. How the tiniest sound echoed. How truly vulnerable she'd be if anyone had a wish to harm her.

"This is the Lord's house," she told herself. "Nobody would…"

Something clicked in the distance. Becky froze, listening. The sound had been so faint she wondered if her imagination was running away with her common sense. This building was like home. As welcoming as her own house. Surely there was no reason to be so jumpy. She never had been before.

Then again, she'd never been aware of her past until yesterday. Remembering chilled her to the core. She was supposed to be the victim, yet she identified so closely with her aunt she felt equally guilty. When had telling the difference between right and wrong gotten so complicated?

Disgusted with the direction her thoughts had taken, she strode quickly to the kitchen in the corner of the basement and began to make coffee for the folks who were expected to attend the meeting.

Noise of running water and the stacking of the

metal filter in the coffee urn covered the natural creaks and groans of the floor overhead, giving Becky a chance to relax.

She began to hum an uplifting tune as she carried the coffeemaker to the pass-through counter, plugged it in and stepped back. "There. All ready."

A door latch clattered upstairs. "Come on down," Becky called. "You're early."

No one answered. No one's steps thumped on the stairs.

She strained to listen. Nothing. But that wasn't a sure sign no one was up there. If Logan's carelessness had resulted in the church being vandalized or burglarized and the culprits were still present, he was certainly going to hear about it.

"I think it's time to call the sheriff."

Reaching into her purse she grabbed her cell phone, ready to dial 911. Common sense stopped her. Half the town listened to police and fire department scanners. How was she going to explain a call for help if there was nothing wrong? The least she could do, before riling everybody up, was tiptoe upstairs and take a peek. As long as she had her phone in hand and the emergency number already dialed in, an SOS could be sent with the push of a button.

Feeling more hesitant with every step, Becky climbed the stairs to the ground floor. The few lights she had turned on when she'd arrived still burned. She looked toward the office. It was dark, as expected, yet soft glimmers of colored light flickered through the doorway and danced against the opposing wall.

She held one finger poised over "call" on her phone, while she reasoned things through. Since Logan had forgotten to lock the outer door, there was a good chance he'd also failed to shut down her computer. The light she was seeing could very well be coming from her screensaver rather than an intruder.

"Hello! Anybody here?" she called before starting down the hall.

Each step closer to the office brought a faster pulse. Shorter, more labored breaths. Unexplainable fear. No matter how often she insisted she was being silly, she couldn't seem to overcome the feeling of foreboding. Of danger.

How many times had she lectured heroines who took foolish chances in movies or on television? Bravado only made sense when a person had a backup plan.

And she had one, she reminded herself. Her grip on the phone tightened. Her thumb rested lightly on the button that would complete her 911 call as she crept closer to the office. The door was ajar. She started to ease it open, stopping dead when she realized what she was seeing.

Her computer was on, all right, but it wasn't the light from the screensaver she'd seen. The computer was apparently logged on to the Internet, or had been, because it was displaying information from one of the search sites she'd used to garner the information on Keringhoven!

Trembling, she peered into the dimly lit office. Shadows seemed to shift, deepen, threaten. Whoever had been there could still be lurking close by. The smartest thing she could do was take the advice she'd given those idiotic heroines in the movies and *run*.

Becky whirled, the small phone clutched to her chest. The toe of her shoe caught on the bottom corner of the half-open door. She stumbled. Her subconscious was screaming that she'd been grabbed by some unseen monster and her conscious mind was too disoriented to argue.

She gasped. Lurched. Started to fall.

Strong arms grabbed her. Becky took a quick breath and let out a screech that echoed from one end of the empty church to the other. Her heart was pounding so hard and fast she could hear it in her ears and sense it in her temples.

The arms held her fast. Unable to regain her balance she hung suspended and kicked wildly.

"Hey! Whoa. It's just me," Logan said. "Cut it out. That hurts."

Becky hit him with the only weapon she had, her telephone. "Let go of me!"

"Gladly." He stepped back, his arms spread wide. "I didn't mean to scare you. I thought you knew I was here."

She staggered, her head swimming. "How would I know that?"

"My car's parked right there," he said, pointing out the window by the side entry. "Next to yours."

"It wasn't there when I got here."

"No." Logan's voice was slow and gentle as if he were speaking to an irrational child. "I arrived after you did. I figured you'd gone to open the front door so I went looking for you there."

"I was in the basement." Becky's gaze swung to the empty office. "Wait a minute. If you just got here, who's been playing with my computer?"

"What?" He scowled.

"My computer. You left the door unlocked and. . ."

"Hold it." He laid a restraining hand on her arm and eased her behind him as if he were a shield. "I didn't leave anything unlocked. I checked all the doors twice before I went home."

"Well, the side door wasn't locked properly."

"Stay right there. Don't move," Logan said.

Barging past her, he switched on all the overhead lights in the office complex and shoved each door open to its fullest, banging them against the walls.

Becky could hardly believe the change in him. Not only was he giving orders like the military policeman he'd once been, his whole demeanor had hardened. Talk about larger-than-life characters from a movie!

She could see that her computer program had now gone to its usual screensaver, which meant that whoever had been running it must have been there within the past ten minutes.

Logan emerged from Fred's office. "This place is clear. I'm going to go check the rest of the church. Lock yourself in till I get back."

"Gladly."

Still shaky, Becky traded places with him and twisted the dead bolt before rounding her desk. If she could end the search program before he returned, he wouldn't have cause to wonder about the unusual name.

That was, of course, assuming he hadn't been the one to look it up in the first place. She hated to admit it but common sense insisted he was the most likely suspect.

The wail of sirens preceded the arrival of flashing red and blue lights atop the sheriff's car.

Though she was still alone, the tension in Becky's shoulders started to ease slightly. Logan must have called the police. He was probably waiting outside to brief them, which would explain why he hadn't returned.

In the distance, several men were shouting. Bracing against the door so she could slam it shut in an emergency, she opened it a crack to listen.

Someone hollered, "Freeze!" followed by thumps and groans. Her heart raced. Had they captured the prowler? Was it safe to open the door? She wished she knew because waiting like this was killing her!

About to succumb to her impatience, she was relieved to hear, "Got him."

Thankful beyond words, she poked her head out of the office. The deputy who stood at the end of the hall guarding the outer door had been one of her classmates in high school. It was an added bonus to see a friendly face.

Grinning, she called, "Hey, Nathan. Fancy meeting you here."

"Stay back, Miss Rebecca. We've got a prowler cornered. Sheriff's bringin' him out now."

"Oh, good."

Her relief was short-lived. The local police had handcuffed Logan Malloy! As the two uniformed men shoved him outside, he shouted, "Becky!"

"Oops." Giggling, she hurried down the hall. "Nathan, wait. That's not a prowler. That's a preacher."

"Hey, Sheriff. Hold on. I think we got the wrong perp," the deputy called.

Becky joined them in time to hear Logan shout, "That's what I've been trying to tell you."

"Then what're you doing with a gun?" the stocky sheriff asked.

"I have a concealed carry permit."

"That wasn't what I asked you, son. I wanna know what a preacher needs with a gun. You care to tell me?"

"No. But if you don't let me go I'll tell my lawyer plenty about false arrest."

"A lawyer?" He reached around behind Logan to free his wrists. "Now what do you need with a lawyer? We're all friendly folks here." Ignoring Logan's muttered reply he turned his attention to Rebecca. "You okay, Miss Becky? When we got your call it sounded like you were scared silly, screamin' and all."

"Me? I never…" She looked back toward the office where all the excitement had begun. Her cell phone was lying on the floor near the door. "Oh, dear. I must have accidentally pushed the button when I ran into Brother Malloy. I'm so sorry."

"You sure about that?" the sheriff drawled, squinting at Logan.

"I'm positive," Becky said. "We were just getting the fellowship hall ready for a meeting and thought we heard noises upstairs. Right, Brother Malloy?"

"That's right." Logan was rubbing his wrists. "And if you two are done with me, I'll go back and finish checking the sanctuary."

"Noises," the sheriff said with a snort. "Right."

Though she'd known the older man since she was a child, she didn't like the inference. She might have been able to convince herself she was imagining his attitude if Nathan hadn't started blushing.

"Yes, *noises*," Becky said with conviction. "There was a prowler in here. He even messed with my computer."

"Well then, let's go see," the sheriff said.

"I—uh—I turned it off." Her admission didn't seem to surprise the lawmen but it clearly shocked Logan.

He glared at her. "You did *what?*"

"I turned it off. I didn't think it was necessary to leave it on."

"How about fingerprints?" Logan asked. "Didn't you think of that?"

"No. I'm not used to being around devious people." Spine stiffening, she made sure the sheriff was looking right at her when she told him, "I don't lie."

The sheriff nodded his acceptance. "Never said

you did, girl. Just doin' my job." His glance settled on Logan, his expression clearly doubtful.

Becky could tell his assessment of truthfulness did *not* extend to Logan Malloy and she had to admit she shared some of the same doubts. Brother Fred might trust Logan implicitly but there was still something about the man that set her nerves on edge.

As soon as the police departed, Logan insisted Becky recheck the office and sanctuary with him to make sure nothing was missing or out of place.

Watching him methodically, cautiously, lead the way through their examination, she started to doubt her earlier conclusions that Logan was the one who had been probing her computer. But if it wasn't him, then who was it?

When she'd used the Internet for her original search she hadn't been worried about anyone else checking to see what sites she'd recently visited. Her personal computer expertise wasn't advanced enough to invade anyone's privacy like that—not that she ever would. However, someone else was obviously smart enough to invade hers.

They'd come full circle. Logan paused in front of the outer office door and placed his hands gently on her shoulders so she had to face him. "Okay. There's no prowler in here now." He sighed heavily. "Promise me you will *never* do that again."

Her first thought was of the computer and her real reasons for shutting it down. "I didn't think about not touching anything. I'm sorry."

"Touching anything?" Logan glanced toward her desk. "Oh, that. Forget it. I was talking about walking into a deserted building when there's a chance it's being burglarized. Don't ever take a chance like that again. Understand?"

"Yes." She nodded and tried to look away, embarrassed by the tears of relief misting her vision.

"Promise?" Logan tipped her chin up with one finger. His tender, concerned reaction confused her. If she didn't know better she'd think he was almost as emotionally disconcerted as she was. "I'm sorry," Becky said. "I'll be more careful next time."

Logan's hand brushed her cheek in a light, brief caress before he pulled away and stepped back. His expression hardened. "There'd better not be a next time."

The homecoming committee meeting was short and productive. Rather than argue, everybody simply deferred to Miss Louella Higgens, who assigned Carol Sue Grabowski to head the booth space group and gave Mercy Cosgrove charge of the food committee, in spite of the elderly woman's polite protest. Leaving the details to Louella made perfect sense to Becky. If a job needed doing, Louella would either handle it herself or draft an unwitting volunteer.

Miss Mercy had brought homemade cookies to go with the coffee, calling for added fellowship after the meeting proper. Logan was chatting with Mercy, leaving Becky a victim of the others' questions.

Louella drew her aside. "What was going on here tonight? I heard sirens."

"It was a false alarm. We thought there was a prowler."

"And?"

"And, we never turned up anybody."

"Who's we? You and Brother Logan?"

"Yes. Why?"

The older woman grinned. "Oh, nothing. It just seemed to some of us that he was spending a lot of extra time with your family. Is old Fred trying to match you two up?"

Becky's eyes widened. "I certainly hope not!"

"Where is Fred tonight, anyway? I expected his input. Homecoming will be here again before we know it."

"He had some hospital visits to make. I doubt he's back in town yet."

"That poor man," Louella crooned. "He's got more miles on him than my old clunker. He deserves his retirement. I'm just not sure how we'll get along without him."

Becky smiled and nodded. "I'm not, either."

"Well, don't you worry," Louella said, emphasizing her comment with a pat on Becky's shoulder, "I'm on the pulpit committee. I'm sure we'll find a good man before Christmas. And he'll be handsome and single. No sense wasting a perfectly good chance to bring new blood into Serenity."

"Louella!"

"Oh, posh. You know as well as I do that there are way too many unmarried women in this church, you among them. Why should we pass up an opportunity like this?"

Becky was chuckling and shaking her head. "I hope you're joking. We need a strong spiritual leader, no matter what his marital status happens to be."

"Okay. I'll go along with that. Who says our future pastor can't be available, too? Certainly not me." She hid a snicker behind her hand. "Look at Brother Logan, for instance. Now there's a good catch for some young woman."

Becky's smile waned. She wouldn't say anything that might taint Logan's already tenuous status in Serenity Chapel, but that didn't keep her from forming her own opinions. Brother Malloy was Fred's close friend, had rescued her off the roof, had protected her from burglars and was doing his best to fill the void Fred's departure would soon create. All of that was in his favor.

On a personal level, however, he was holding too much back for her to view him as a good marriage prospect, assuming she was looking for a husband, which she certainly wasn't. The man was too mysterious. Too reclusive when it came to details about himself or his past. He was too…

She glanced across the room, meaning only to reinforce her conclusions that Logan was many things, all of them troubling. He was openly staring at her.

Though she quickly turned away and began straightening up the kitchen, Becky felt his eyes continuing to follow her every move.

By the time she managed to usher everyone out the door so that she could lock up, she was a nervous wreck. Plus, she was mad at herself for taking the situation so to heart.

Must be leftover anxiety from the prowler scare, she decided as she headed for the parking lot with the others.

Recalling that episode intensified her edginess.

There was still the unanswered question of who had been fooling with her computer. If it truly hadn't been Logan, then who had it been? And why?

Chapter Eleven

Becky wished she hadn't disposed of her original list of the Keringhoven contacts she'd found on the Internet. Not having a computer at home meant she'd have to use the one at work again if she wanted to replace those phone numbers and renew her search now that she had more information.

Before she did anything, however, she intended to learn how to guard against prying eyes, which meant a visit to someone more knowledgeable than she was. The first person who came to mind was Belinda Randall.

Office hours for the chamber of commerce were the only complication. If Becky aimed to sneak off to visit her friend during the day she'd have to do it at lunchtime.

Rather than share her plans with Brother Fred and give him another chance to suggest she take Logan along, Becky left a note on her desk, grabbed her purse and was out the door at eleven-thirty sharp.

Logan heard her car start and drive away. He raised an eyebrow at Fred. "I think our chicken has flown the coop."

The older man chuckled. "You're beginning to sound like the rest of us country folks."

"Never." Logan snorted. "Next thing you know, you'll be asking me to preach."

"Why not? You're ordained."

"I'm also seriously out of practice."

"So?"

"So, it's not my calling. I've told you that before."

"You also told me you were happy being a private investigator."

"I am."

The old man cocked his head and raised a gray eyebrow in contradiction. "Are you? I wonder. Can you honestly tell me you haven't started to feel like you've come home since you've been here?"

Logan rose and paced across the office before answering. "If I do feel like that, it's because of you, not because of the job. It's been good to see you again."

"And you're telling yourself that's a lucky accident?" Fred asked wisely.

"What else could it be?" Logan raised his hands, palms out. "Oh, no. You're not going to suggest this was all meant to be, are you?"

"Why not? You said it yourself. If you hadn't stumbled on this case in the first place, your client might have sent people who would have torn this town apart."

"That doesn't mean it was all providential."

"No," Fred said. "But it sure does point to that conclusion. If you weren't so stubborn you might be able to see the writing on the wall." He smiled. "Don't forget what happened to old Belshazzar when he didn't pay attention. He lost everything."

"I have nothing to lose," Logan countered.

Fred smiled. "I wouldn't be so sure."

"I need to find out how to hide the sites I've visited if I use the office computer to look things up on the Internet," Becky told Belinda.

"Why? What are you checking that's so secret?"

Becky was sorely tempted to confide in her friend. Perhaps she would—later. "Don't look at me like that. I'm not doing anything wrong. I think somebody's been fooling with my computer when I'm not there and I need to safeguard the data files."

"So, set up a password."

"That might help at night. During the day we usually leave everything up and running. Anybody could use my desk if I stepped away."

"Anybody?" The dark-haired woman was scowling. "Who's there besides you and Brother Fred." Her eyes widened. "Ah-ha. Has Brother Malloy been giving you trouble?"

"I don't think it was him. He said it wasn't."

"You believe him?"

"I want to." Becky made a silly face. "I've been trying to treat him the same way I do Fred. Can't say that's working very well, though."

"Surprise, surprise," Belinda drawled.

"Stop leering. I know what everybody thinks. It's not true. Brother Logan and I are hardly even friends. That's part of the problem."

"You don't like him?"

"I didn't say that."

"Then what's bothering you?"

Becky shook her head and pressed her lips into a thin line while she considered the question. "He asks too many questions."

"What's wrong with that? Lots of people are curious by nature."

"I suppose so."

Thoughtful, Becky strolled to the window of the chamber office and gazed at passersby. Older folks were lounging in the sun on benches that framed the courthouse lawn. The usual complement of farmers, ranchers and merchants was going in and out of the courthouse on business. Children too young for school were playing hide-and-seek around the gazebo on the southwest corner.

Everything seemed normal but *her*—and the two men she'd just noticed standing next to a shiny black car parked across the street. They were trying to act nonchalant but their clothing gave them away. It was too citified, too *GQ*. And the black car was far too clean to have traveled the dirt roads in and around Serenity.

Becky motioned to Belinda. "Come here a sec. Do you know those guys?"

"Nope. Never seen 'em before. Have you?"

"I'm not sure. I may have. Guess I'm just jumpy after last night."

"I heard there was quite a commotion at the church."

"Everybody in town probably knows about it by now." She shivered and wrapped her arms around herself.

"Was there really a prowler?"

"I don't know. We never found anybody. I'd gone to open the fellowship hall for a meeting when I thought I heard noises upstairs. If Logan hadn't been there, too, I'd have bailed out and waited for the police."

"What did you do?"

"Locked myself in the office while Logan searched the place from top to bottom."

"That was stupid, if you don't mind my saying so. He was risking your life as well as his own."

"Yes and no," Becky explained. "He used to be an MP." She lowered her voice to add, "And he was armed."

"Armed? You mean he had a *gun?*" Belinda sounded astonished. "On him? In church?"

Becky huffed. "Yeah. The sheriff was surprised, too. Brother Logan had a permit to carry a concealed weapon so nothing came of it."

"The guy must have come from a pretty tough area. I'm glad I'm not a part of *that* congregation."

"I know what you mean. My heart tells me I should love every believer, no matter what their background, but my head keeps arguing for self-preservation. I think that's part of my problem with Brother Logan. He makes me nervous."

Belinda began to smile. "Oh? You mean tingly all over and butterflies in your stomach? Chills? Shakes? Dry mouth?"

"Yes, but don't go making more out of it than there really is, okay?"

Laughing, the slightly older woman put her arm around Becky's shoulders, gave her a squeeze and led her away from the window. "Honey, that's not up to me. Sounds like you've got it bad, whether you're ready to admit it or not. I think you're in love."

"No way. I hardly know the man." Becky twisted free and distanced herself from her friend. "He scares me."

"Okay. If you say so."

"I do."

"Fine." Belinda led the way to her computer terminal and sat in front of the monitor. "While I show you how to access your history and change preferences on the main program, you can decide exactly what you're afraid of."

"I'm afraid I'll erase data, among other things."

"I wasn't referring to the computer, Becky, I was talking about you. I suspect you're a lot more scared of your own feelings than you are of Logan Malloy."

Becky opened her mouth to protest, then snapped it closed without saying a word.

The private line on Brother Fred's desk rang just after one. Logan was alone in the office. The minute he answered with the words, "Serenity Chapel," Becky started babbling.

"They're after me!"

"Who is?"

"Logan? Is that you? Oh, thank God," she said

prayerfully. "Two men were loitering outside the chamber office. They followed me when I left. They're still behind me!"

Logan gripped the receiver. "Are you sure?"

"Positive."

"Okay. Calm down. Where are you now?"

"On 62-412, going west. I'd planned to stop at the post office."

"Don't," Logan said firmly. "Stick to well-traveled streets and come straight back here. Don't speed or take chances. And whatever happens, don't let them force you off the road."

"Maybe I'm imagining things."

"And maybe you're not. Are they still behind you?"

"Yes. I'll turn back toward the square and see what happens." In seconds she added, "They turned, too!"

"Okay. Stay cool. I'm going to break this connection and call you back on my cell phone so I'll be mobile, too. Hang up and wait for my call."

Logan hoped and prayed she wasn't too distressed to follow his orders. He hated to stop talking to her but if she needed his help, he'd have to be able to take directions on the move.

Running for his car, he punched her name on the speed dial. He was slamming the door of the red convertible when she answered.

"Logan?"

"It's me. I'm leaving the church now. Which direction?"

"Make a right. Go to the signal and turn right again. "I should get to the square about the same time you do." She hesitated for a few heartbeats. "The other car is big and black. A Caddy or something like that. I noticed it first because it was too clean. It didn't fit in."

"Gotcha. I'm on my way. Stay on the line."

He arrived at the traffic signal in seconds. It was red. Logan banged his fist on the steering wheel, then spoke into his phone. "You still there? I'm stuck at the light."

"I'm here," Becky answered. "So far, so good. I've passed the old Laundromat on Church Street and I'm almost to the grocery store."

"Are your friends still with you?"

"Oh, yeah. They haven't tried to catch me, though."

"Good." Logan made the turn. "Okay. I'm moving again. Which side of the square shall I take?"

"Go straight, past the courthouse, then left at the pet store. We should pass each other in that block."

Logan heard her fumble, grumble and recover. "Sorry. I dropped the phone. I see your car. What should I do?"

"Go back to the church and lock yourself in."

"Wait a minute. What about you? What are you going to do?"

"Talk to your new friends. Or try to."

"Be careful."

He was touched by the concern in her voice. "I won't take chances as long as I know you're safe."

Nodding acknowledgement as she passed, he pulled wide, cut the wheel tight to the left, and slid the convertible into a U-turn in the middle of the street. The sound of his squealing tires drew plenty of attention. That couldn't be helped. By the time the black car passed a few seconds later, Logan was headed in the right direction to slip in behind it.

He hadn't recognized the faces of the driver or passenger. He had, however, recognized their type. They were cheap hired hands, maybe bounty hunters, though he doubted it. If he'd had to guess, he would have started by assuming they were flunkies sent to hurry his cautious investigation. Chances were good Keringhoven had carried out the threat to bring in additional investigators, and if that were the case, he was going to have to intervene in order to protect Becky.

How had he gotten on the other side of this? Logan suddenly wondered. The answer was basic. He'd chosen the side of innocence; the side he'd begun to care for. Nobody was going to hurt Rebecca Tate if he could help it, starting with the guys in the black car.

Logan hung back, letting them get several car lengths ahead. He was close enough to see Becky turn in at the church driveway.

He picked up his phone. "So far, so good. Keep going. I won't follow you all the way up unless they do."

There was a short pause. "I think it's okay, Logan. They just drove by."

"I know. I'm right behind them. Go on in and lock the door, like I told you."

"What about you?"

"I'll be back soon."

"Wait! What if they're just tourists or something?"

"Then they're going to get the kind of welcome you southerners are *not* used to handing out. Leave the rough stuff to us Yankees."

"That's not funny," she said. "I don't want you or anybody else causing trouble on my account."

"Then think of it as retribution. They followed you and scared you. The least I can do is return the favor."

"Logan!"

The line went dead.

* * *

Becky's first inclination was to turn around and go after him. That was such a dumb idea she immediately talked herself out of it, which left following his orders, like it or not.

Muttering to herself, she entered the chapel building and flipped the dead bolt inside the main door.

"Okay. Now what?" she asked the empty air.

No answer was forthcoming. Her cell phone was still clutched in her hand. Knowing that Logan would probably try to contact her that way again, she took it with her to the office where she dialed her aunt on a landline.

Each ring of the unanswered phone made her heart beat faster. She was about to hang up when Effie barked, "You better not be sellin' anything. I'm in the middle of bakin' cookies."

"Aunt Effie, it's me. Are you all right?"

"'Course I am. Why wouldn't I be?"

"I was just checking on you."

"Don't give me that, Rebecca. I know you too well. Something's wrong. What is it?"

"Nothing. Really." She was rapidly realizing she shouldn't have contacted Effie until she'd calmed down more. There was no easy way to explain what had occurred without unduly upsetting the older woman. Given Effie's tenuous mental state, stories about being chased by strangers were definitely out of the question.

"Who's been telling you tales about me this time?" Effie asked.

"Nobody. I just had a minute and thought I'd give you a call." She changed the subject. "What kind of cookies are you baking?"

"Oatmeal with raisins. Fred's favorite. I figured to take him some when I got done. Thelma can drive me."

"Don't do that," Becky said abruptly. "Brother Fred's not here. I don't have a clue when he'll be back, either. Why don't you and I deliver the cookies to him later?"

"Well…"

Becky could tell there was still too much emotion behind her responses. For Effie's sake, she fought the urge to confess everything the way she used to when she was a little girl, though she wondered if it was wise to continue to keep her aunt in the dark about what had just happened. Would she be taking a chance with the old woman's safety if she didn't warn her?

Warn her about what? Surely there wasn't anything serious going on. Becky shivered, remembering Effie's recent ramblings about unseen danger. Was paranoia catching? If it was, she'd apparently been infected all the way to the roots of her hair because it was prickling at her nape.

She made a snap decision. "Look, Aunt Effie. You stay put and finish your baking. I'll run home for a few minutes and explain everything. Okay?" There was no response. "Okay, Aunt Effie?"

The receiver clattered as if it had been dropped. When it was picked up again, Effie said, "I'm back."

"Why didn't you answer me just now? Where were you? You scared me to death."

"I went to lock the doors," the older woman said in a subdued tone. "Hurry home. I'll be waiting."

Chapter Twelve

Logan was frustrated. He'd been hot on the trail of the black car and about to intercept it until an enormous green tractor hauling a set of implements had pulled out ahead of him. The lumbering rig had taken up most of both sides of the roadway. By the time Logan had found a place to pass, his quarry was long gone.

Already on edge, he headed the few miles back to Serenity, roared into the church parking lot and skidded to a stop. Eyes wide, he swallowed past the lump in his throat. Becky's car wasn't there!

He immediately tried to telephone her. Inside the building, a phone rang.

Straight-arming the door, he raced down the hall. His heart fell. Her cell phone was ringing all right.

She'd left it lying on her desk. Wherever she'd gone, he wouldn't be able to contact her that way. Worse, she'd left in such a hurry she hadn't remembered to lock the door. That was so totally out of character for her it gave him chills.

Logan slammed the side of his fist into the doorjamb, trying to mute his fury and decide on his next move. The black car had gotten away so he had no idea if Becky had been right about being followed. Since she was now missing, he had to assume she was in further jeopardy. As frightened as she'd sounded, it was hard to believe she'd disregarded his good advice and left the church without being forced to.

"Unless she was worried about somebody else," Logan muttered. He grabbed her cell phone. The last number it had dialed was his. He threw it down, snatched up the desk phone and pushed the redial button.

A shaky voice said, "Hello?"

"Effie? Is that you?" he demanded.

"Who is this?"

"Logan Malloy. Brother Malloy," he said quickly. "I'm looking for Becky. Is she there?"

To his astonishment, there was a click on the line. Logan stared at the receiver. The old woman had hung up on him! What that meant was anybody's guess, although he'd long suspected Effie Tate wasn't nearly as addlebrained as she pretended to be.

Leaving Becky's cell phone on her desk in case she retuned for it, he hurried back to his car. He was beginning to understand the rustic analogy about running around like a chicken with its head cut off. He was certainly feeling plenty brainless and undirected at the moment.

Every instinct screamed at him to slow down. To think. To plan. To gather more information before rushing off to Effie's house like an idiot. But his emotions overruled his good sense. Becky might be in trouble. She might need him. He had to go to her.

That was all he could think about. The only course of action his heart and mind would accept.

Effie opened the front door to her niece as soon as Becky arrived, then locked it behind her. Though Becky was breathless and agitated, the older woman seemed completely in control.

"I told you," Effie said. "For years I told you. *Now* do you believe me?"

"About what?" Becky was still trying to quiet her pounding heart.

"Strangers. They're here. I seen 'em. One called, too, but I hung up on him."

"Are you sure?"

The gray head nodded sagely. "Sure as the world."

"Maybe you'd better sit down." She managed a smile. "Actually, maybe *I'd* better sit down. I feel kind of shaky."

Effie led the way to the kitchen. The aroma of freshly baked cookies made the room seem so welcoming, so safe, it was hard for Becky to stay focused on her earlier concerns. Still, there was nothing imaginary about the men who had followed her all over town. Something odd was definitely going on. And since none of this had started until after her calls to the people named Keringhoven, she had to assume that was in some way tied to their present predicament.

She eyed her aunt. The elderly eyes were bright, clear, piercing in their intensity. If there was ever a good time for probing questions, this was it.

Taking a seat at the table she cleared her throat. "Um, Aunt Effie? Please sit down. I need to ask you something. It's about my past. Our past. What does it have to do with anyone named Keringhoven?"

A long pause. "Nothing."

If Effie's shoulders hadn't slumped like a marionette whose strings had been cut, Becky might have believed her. She reached across the table and grasped her aunt's thin hands. "Please? I found an old photo and I wondered…"

"Where? Where'd you find it?"

"In the trunk in the garage. I was looking for the quilt top you started when I was little. I was going to try to finish it before Christmas and surprise you."

Tears glistened. "Show me that picture."

Becky went to her room and returned. She laid the faded snapshot on the table in front of her aunt. "Here. I look so much like the woman I thought we must be related. Is that my mother? The one you told me about?"

Effie nodded. Her hands were trembling as she gently touched the image. "Yes. That's Flo."

"Was her maiden name Tate?"

"No." Slowly, hesitantly, she looked up. Tears welled. "Effie Tate was a girlhood friend of mine. She died when we were both very young."

Becky sank to her knees beside the old woman and once again reached for her frail hands. "Then who are you? And who am I?"

Instead of answering, Effie pulled away, folded her arms, put her head down on the table and began to sob uncontrollably.

The banging at Becky's front door was so violent it shook the house. If she hadn't recognized Logan's shouts of "Open up!" she'd have met him at the door swinging their heaviest iron frying pan as a defensive weapon.

She hated to leave Effie crying like that but she didn't want the neighbors to panic and call the police over Logan's assault on the door. One false alarm featuring her and their substitute preacher was plenty.

"Hold your horses," she yelled back. "I'm coming."

When she opened the door she could see he was livid. Not only was his face flushed, his gaze was piercing. She stepped back. "You want to come in, or are you going to stand out there and holler at me all day?"

"I haven't even begun to yell," Logan said, shouldering through the doorway. He wheeled. "Where were you? Why didn't you stay at the office like I told you to? Were you trying to give me a heart attack?"

"No, of course not. I just..." There was moisture gathering in his eyes! His expression touched her soul. The man might be hard as nails on the outside but there was no denying his kindhearted, compassionate inner nature.

Becky reached to caress his cheek, to impress upon him how truly sorry she was. The fervor in his gaze seemed to darken, intensify. Her hand sank to his chest as he reached out and drew her closer.

"Do you have any idea what you did to me?" he whispered against her hair. "I went crazy when I couldn't find you."

She laid her cheek on his chest. "I'm so sorry. I didn't mean to make you worry. I got to thinking about Aunt Effie, being here all alone, and I knew I had to see for myself that she was okay."

Logan kissed the top of her head, his lips lingering. "I know what you mean."

What was he saying? That he cared for her as much as she cared about Effie? It had sounded that way. Then again, he'd suffered a fright and could be overreacting.

Such a logical train of thought struck Becky as ironic. There was certainly nothing levelheaded about the way she was beginning to feel about Logan Malloy. Even if Belinda was right and she was falling in love with him, it still didn't make any sense. Of all the men she knew, he was the least likely to bring her happiness. They had nothing in common, except their faith and a fondness for Brother Fred, and that didn't seem like a very firm foundation on which to build a life together.

She sighed. Snuggled closer. Listened to the beating of Logan's heart and smiled. Never mind the future. Being in his arms was not only amazingly comforting, it was just the kind of support she needed right now. Tomorrow would have to take care of itself. She was busy enjoying today. So much so, in fact, that she leaned back slightly and lifted her face to him.

Logan loosened his embrace and eased her away. "No, Becky," he said hoarsely. "Don't."

She knew he was thinking of kissing her because the same notion had taken up residence in her mind. "We have a chaperone. Aunt Effie's in the kitchen."

"You don't know me."

That brought a deep, noisy sigh. "Well, Brother Malloy, I hate to tell you this, but I'm not very well-acquainted with myself, either."

"What do you mean?" He started to ease away.

"It's a long story. I just found out that Aunt Effie isn't a Tate. Neither am I. It's no wonder her mind gave out. I can't imagine hiding a secret like that for so many years."

"How do you know she's not just confused again?"

Becky took his warm, comforting hand and started to lead him toward the kitchen. "Because I have a picture to prove it. Come on. I'll show you."

Logan didn't need urging to accompany her. He was so relieved to have found her alive and well he wouldn't have left her side if the house had caught fire.

When her hand tightened on his he thought she was being affectionate until he noticed that the kitchen was empty. No wonder he'd been subconsciously thinking of fire! Smoke was beginning to seep out of the oven and billow into the room. A smoke alarm started to beep.

Becky grabbed a potholder and rescued the charred sheet of cookies, then turned on the vent hood over the stove. She was about to start for the back door till she noticed that Logan had already thrown it open.

One quick scan of the smoky room told her that both Effie and the photograph were missing. She clutched at Logan's arm. "Effie's gone!"

"Evidently. Could she have forgotten she was baking?"

"It's never happened before."

He was about to suggest they search the house when Becky bolted past him. He waited in the hallway while she ran through each bedroom. By the time she rejoined him, her eyes were wide and her already fair skin was ashen.

"She's not here?" Logan asked.

Becky shook her head. "But why would she leave? I know she was afraid to go out."

"Maybe she was more afraid of staying here after I arrived," he said. "She never has liked me. I almost scared her into pitching off the roof the first time we met."

"I'm sorry to say you're right." Becky was wringing her hands. Her gaze was darting from the inside of the house to the windows and doors. "She can't have gone far. Even if she hadn't lost her driver's license the last time she took the test, she was too beside herself to drive."

"We should check with the neighbors first," Logan said.

"Right." Becky raced to the door and paused only long enough to point. "You take Miss Mercy's. I'll check Thelma's."

Logan was jogging across the lawn when he skidded to a stop. "Becky!"

She glanced over her shoulder. "What?"

"Come back. I know what happened to your aunt."

"What?" She froze.

Logan was shaking his head while standing in the driveway beside Becky's car. It was the only vehicle present. "Why did Effie flunk her driving test?" he shouted.

"Bad peripheral vision," Becky answered. "Why?"

"Because, she stole my car."

Brother Fred Fleming had been visiting the local nursing home and was on his way out. He wasn't surprised to see a familiar red convertible approaching. He nearly swallowed his dentures, however, when he recognized the diminutive woman behind the wheel.

Effie skidded to a stop practically at his feet. She jammed the car into Park and jumped out, hollering, "Praise the Lord! I found you."

If Fred hadn't been braced she might have bowled him over when she threw herself into his arms. "Take it easy, Miss Effie. What's wrong? Is Becky hurt?"

"No," Effie said with breathlessness and rancor, "but that Logan Malloy is about to get the best of me." She paused long enough to take a few shaky breaths, then plunged ahead. "Rebecca found out who we really are. She must of told him, 'cause he showed up at the house right after."

"Who you really are? I don't understand." Fred's voice was little above a whisper.

Effie continued to babble. "She showed me a picture of her and Flo and the others. I knew I should of burned it. But it was the only picture I had of her mama and I thought maybe someday she'd want it. I never dreamed it'd stir up all this trouble."

Keeping his arm around her shoulders, he guided her away from Logan's car and toward his own. "What do you say you and I go for a ride and talk? Sort this all out by ourselves?"

"Suits me," Effie said. "I've got plenty to say."

"I wish you'd confided in me years ago," Fred said gently.

"I wish I had, too. Maybe now you'll see why I couldn't marry you, no matter how I felt. It wouldn't have been fair, you bein' a preacher and all."

Nodding, Fred said, "I knew there had to be more to it than you'd let on. Why couldn't you have trusted me?"

"Because you were too honorable." There was a catch in her voice. "If you'd married me and then found out what I'd done, you'd have had to turn me in. Your conscience would have made you. I know it and so do you."

"I'm still the same person," Fred said.

"But the girl's not a helpless baby anymore." Effie sniffled, swiped at her tears in frustration. "She can stand on her own. She knows what kind of a man her father is and she can tell him she doesn't want anything to do with the likes of him."

"Is he that bad?"

She snorted in disgust. "Bad? Guess so. He killed her poor mama. And maybe her brother, too."

Chapter Thirteen

Becky and Logan had located his car, abandoned at the rest home, and had decided to leave it there for the present. By evening, the only place they hadn't checked was Fred's new home on Lake Norfork because they lacked an exact address.

Becky was driving. She pulled over and stopped on the shoulder of the highway. "We have some decisions to make."

"For instance?"

"Do we keep driving around like we have been or do we go home and wait for Aunt Effie to turn up?"

"She's your aunt. What would you like to do?"

"Right now?" Becky gave a quiet, "Humph," then said, "I don't know. Scream? Tear my hair? Cry? Pick one."

"Are those my only choices?" Logan asked with a lopsided smile.

"Probably. They seem to be mine."

He laid his hand over hers, meaning to offer comfort. There was unspoken compassion in the act, in his heart. When she looked at him, however, he saw a more complicated mix of emotions, especially in the glistening blue of her eyes. Her lips were parted slightly. The lower one quivered.

Logan knew he'd be ten times the fool if he gave in and put his arms around her. He also knew he was losing the battle to hold himself in check. He started to lean toward her. Their warm breath mingled. Logan imagined he could already taste the sweetness of her kiss.

Becky laid her fingertips against his lips. "Wait. There's something I have to tell you."

Her words splashed like icy water over his ardor. He straightened, pulled away. "All right."

"It's about Aunt Effie and me," she said slowly, deliberately. "Remember what I said about not being a real Tate?"

"Vaguely." Logan's gut twisted.

"Well, I don't understand it all yet, but apparently Aunt Effie changed our names when she adopted me. She said she was afraid of my father, only…" Becky paled. "Wait a minute. If my mother was killed and my father disappeared and doesn't care, like she told me, then why would she be so afraid?"

"Maybe your father does care."

"Could he?"

"Anything's possible." Logan wanted desperately to confess his part in the subterfuge. He took her hand. "Listen. There's something I need to say, too."

The faraway look in her eyes told him she wasn't paying attention. No wonder. The safe little world she'd grown up in had been fractured by her aunt's partial confession. Once Becky got all the facts and realized how badly she'd been deceived by the person she loved most, she was going to be devastated. This was clearly not the time for him to clear his own conscience and add to her misery.

Logan got out of the car and circled around it, opening the driver's door. "Scoot over. I'll drive you home."

Her lack of objection told him he'd made the right choice when he'd held his peace. Poor Becky was bewildered, as well she should be. It wasn't every day a supposed orphan figured out she might have a surviving parent.

And if that news had stunned her, wait till she learned the rest.

* * *

Brother Fred's tan car was parked in the Tate driveway when Logan pulled up in front of the house.

Becky leaped out and ran toward the front door. She burst in before Logan could catch up to her. "Aunt Effie?" Her vision misted in relief when she spotted her aunt. "I thought I'd lost you."

Effie was seated on the sofa. Brother Fred left his place beside her and motioned for Becky to take it. "Here. You two have a lot to talk about," Fred said. "We'll wait outside so you can have some privacy."

He caught Logan's arm and urged him to back off. "Come on, son. I'll tell you all about it."

Loathe to leave Becky, Logan resisted. "Are you sure?"

"Positive," his mentor assured him. "They need a few minutes alone. It'll be all right."

Logan refused to go farther than the front porch. "This'll do. I think there are other operatives in the area. Guys I don't know. We shouldn't leave the women unguarded."

"Our prowler?" Fred asked.

"Probably. Whoever he was, he was interested in what was stored in Becky's computer files. I'm positive somebody had been snooping around her office."

"That wasn't *your* doing?" Fred asked soberly.

"No. If it had been, I wouldn't have been careless enough to have left the information displayed. I'm sure she's the missing Keringhoven baby. I just haven't decided what to do about it."

"Maybe what I have to say will help you make up your mind." Fred sighed. "Effie's explained everything."

"Go on."

"Not until I have your word you won't act without taking it all into careful consideration."

Logan scowled. "I'm already doing that."

"You're right. You are."

Waiting for Fred to speak seemed to take eons. Logan forced himself to take deep, settling breaths and bide his time when what he wanted to do was shout at the older man to get on with it.

Finally, the story began. "Effie was the nanny, just like Keringhoven told you. She was in charge of both children, baby Rebecca and her older brother, Cody. Florence had been an unhappy wife and mother for a long time but she'd stuck it out. Effie was her confidante. That's how she learned about the physical abuse."

"He beat his wife?" Logan had considered himself a good judge of character and was astounded he'd misjudged the man so badly. Then again, a lot of years had passed since Becky's disappearance. People could change.

"That's what Effie told me," Fred said sadly. "Flo was too afraid of her husband to leave him lawfully, so the two women planned an escape. They were going to run away together and take the children."

"That would have been legal. Messy, but legal."

"I know." The old man's shoulders slumped. He sat down on the porch and leaned forward, elbows on his knees, fingers laced. "Only Flo never made it."

"Right. There was an accident and she was killed. That's all in the file."

Nodding, Fred stared at his clasped hands. "Suppose the crash wasn't an accident? Effie thinks Flo was murdered."

"No way." Logan began to pace the porch. "There was an investigation. The woman drove her car into a bridge abutment. If it wasn't a mistake, it was suicide."

"That was my first thought. But Effie's positive Flo was looking forward to her freedom. Effie had already gone into hiding with the baby. Flo was supposed to bring the older child, Cody, and join them. When she didn't show up, Effie panicked and ran. She was thinking of going back until she heard Flo was dead."

"So she kept running."

"Exactly."

Sighing, Fred looked at Logan, silently pleading for understanding and sympathy. "She figured she'd be caught unless she changed her name, so she got the birth certificate of a childhood friend and assumed her identity. That only left what to do about the baby. She bribed somebody to falsify a birth certificate. How she got away with that is a mystery, but she did."

"If Keringhoven was so bad, how could she stand to leave the little boy behind?"

"That tore her up. It still does. But she knew she didn't dare try to rescue him, too. If she had, she could very easily have lost Becky."

"Unbelievable."

"That's what I said when she told me." He rose. "So, what are you going to do? Go to the police?"

"I should," Logan said flatly. "Laws were broken. People were hurt."

"Is there any hurry after all this time?" Brother Fred asked. "Can't you take awhile? Probe a little deeper? Make sure you have the right information?"

That had already occurred to Logan and he'd come to the conclusion he was up against an immense challenge, both to his secular principles and to his faith. Separating the two was getting harder and harder. If he didn't eventually reveal Effie's crime, he'd be abdicating his vow to uphold the law. If he turned her in too soon, however, he might be thwarting the Lord's plans for this sticky situation. Far be it from him to assume he knew the mind of God, especially this time.

"I'll give it some thought," Logan finally said. "I won't make my move without consulting you first. Will that be good enough?"

Fred rose and shook his hand, clapping him on the shoulder at the same time. "I couldn't ask for more. Come on. I'll drive you back so you can pick up your car. It won't take us five minutes."

Becky was thunderstruck. It was as if all her fantasies about happy family life had been melted in the fires of reality. No wonder Aunt Effie was so distrustful of men. After all she'd been through, who wouldn't be?

It was hard for Becky to believe her father could have purposely caused her mother's death. The whole story seemed unreal, impossible, though it did explain a lot of things she'd wondered about ever since she'd gotten old enough to ask questions. Questions like, where did her parents live? How had they died? Did she have any other living relatives?

The fanciful stories Effie had told about their

family had been far-fetched and changeable, leading
Becky to doubt them all. Now, her reasons for telling tales made sense in a sad sort of way.

If Effie was being truthful this time, she and
Becky weren't even remotely related. That was the
harshest truth of all.

Though she didn't want to admit any change in
her affection, Becky noticed an emotional distancing that made her heart ache with loss.

She took Effie's hand and squeezed it as she said,
"I need to get away. Take a walk by myself. Think
things through. Will you be okay?"

Effie nodded. "I'd like to see Brother Fred again.
Would you ask him to come back inside, please?"

"Of course."

Rising, Becky walked slowly to the door, opened
it, and stepped onto the porch. Fred and Logan had
just returned and greeted her with expectant looks.
She managed a smile. "Effie wants to see you again,
Brother Fred, if you don't mind."

"Not at all." After a brief glance at the younger
man, he went back into the house.

Left alone with Logan, Becky stood tall, chin up.
"You heard?"

"Fred filled me in. I'm sorry."

"Boy, me, too," she said. "When I said I didn't
know myself, I didn't realize how right I was!"

"What are you going to do now? Look for your father?"

Her brow furrowed. "Why would I want to do that?"

"I don't know. Maybe for Effie's sake."

"It's for her sake that I won't. I made the mistake of looking into the past once. I don't intend to make it again."

"What about your brother?"

Becky cocked her head and studied his expression. "Effie assumes he's dead. Why would you think otherwise?"

"Logic," Logan said with a shrug. "She obviously heard plenty about your mother's accident. Why not keep tabs on the family to find out how the boy was doing?"

"I think she was afraid to," Becky explained. "She's still beating herself up about not rescuing him. If she'd learned anything bad about him, in a newspaper or whatever, it might have driven her over the edge."

"You mean before now?"

"Yes. I'm no doctor, but I'm beginning to think the cause of her mental lapses may be more because of guilt than because of aging brain cells."

"How long has it been since she's seen a doctor?"

Becky purposely refrained from mentioning

Fred's recent attempt at intervention via his chaplain friend. "Not long. Since all this has come out, I'm going to make sure she sees her regular doctor soon, though."

"And then what? Confess?" Logan asked. "Think for a second. Are you sure you want Effie to come clean to everybody the way she did to you and Fred?"

"Well…"

He cupped Becky's elbow and guided her off the porch, lowering his voice when he finally paused at the edge of the street. "I wouldn't encourage it. Not yet. Make a doctor's appointment if you want, but keep the sordid details of your aunt's story to yourself, at least until we're sure what really happened. I'll make a few calls, look into it for you."

"Thanks. I suppose you're right." Becky looked up at him with appreciation. "The fewer the people who know, the better off we'll all be, especially poor Effie." She smiled slightly and reached for his hand. "I'm glad you're here. Fred's too close to Aunt Effie to see things clearly. He may need your counsel."

Who's going to counsel me? Logan wondered. *Who's going to tell me how to get out of this mess without hurting the only woman who's ever been this important to me?*

This was a foxhole moment. The kind of epiphany he'd had as a young soldier afraid of making the wrong move. Or as a seminary graduate questioning his career choices. Each instance had been bathed in prayer, yet he hadn't been nearly as certain then as he was right now.

He'd come to Serenity thinking he was working for a man, when in reality he'd been working for the Lord. Perhaps he'd never stopped, even when he'd left the pulpit to follow a different path.

That conclusion settled in his heart and cocooned him in peace.

Fred was right. It did feel like coming home.

Chapter Fourteen

Continuing to go to work every day as if nothing had changed seemed surreal to Becky. If the truth were told, her emotions were in such an upheaval she could hardly think straight, let alone work efficiently.

The urge to confide in her friend Belinda or one of the women from her Sunday school class was strong. Stronger still was the gut-level warning she kept getting every time she considered saying anything to anyone other than Fred or Logan.

Fred had been spending most of his free time with Effie. They'd sat at the Tate kitchen table, talking and drinking coffee, for hours every evening. When Becky had awakened at 2:00 a.m. the night before, they were still at it. She knew she should be happy for them, but she couldn't help wondering

what was going to happen to their renewed closeness, if and when Effie had to pay for her crime. That
thought sent shivers skittering along her spine like
a dry leaf tumbling in a gale.

Logan was passing her desk. He hesitated. "You
okay?"

"Fine. I was just thinking."

"I thought I saw steam coming out of your ears."

"Couldn't be that." She made a silly face. "Steam
is for when you're mad. The way I've been grinding
my gears, I think smoke is more likely."

"At least it wasn't as bad as burning cookies."

Becky chuckled. "I hope not. If it looks like it's
getting worse, don't call the fire department, okay?"

"Okay." Logan laughed with her and settled a hip
on the edge of her desk. "How's Effie doing?"

"As good as can be expected, I guess. Have you
found out anything about my family?"

"A little. It turns out your brother Cody is alive
and well. He was secure in the back seat when
your mother had her accident. Didn't get a
scratch."

"That's wonderful." She studied his closed expression and decided he was hiding something. An
eyebrow arched. "Okay, out with it. What else?"

"Nothing else, for now."

"Oh, no, you don't." Becky stood to face him.

Since he was still half seated, they were close to eye-level. She put her hands on his shoulders to keep him there while she made her demands. "I want to know it all. Right now. No glossing over, no holding back. Got that?"

Logan didn't look pleased. "Where's Fred when a guy needs him?"

"Probably with my counterfeit aunt," Becky said. "If you know that much about my brother, you should know whether Effie was telling the truth about everything else."

"She was," Logan said with a sigh. "At least the truth as she believed it." He placed his hands at Becky's waist. "There's more. I'm just not sure you're ready to hear it."

"I'm ready, believe me. *More* than ready. Now give, mister, or I'll conk you with the door again, like I did when we first met in Brother Fred's office."

He laughed quietly, appreciatively. "You're quite a lady, Miss Rebecca."

"Well, at least your Southern accent is improving. Come on. Talk. I may be easygoing about most things but I've never been accused of having too much patience."

Nodding, he gazed into her eyes, hoping she'd accept what he had to say without misunderstanding. "I do know more about your father. His name is Dan

Keringhoven. He's been searching for you for years without any luck. He had no idea your mother was unhappy, so when she took off with your brother and wrecked her car, it was a shock."

"That's not what Effie said."

"I know. Bear with me for a minute. After you and Effie disappeared, he started checking with your mother's friends and discovered she'd been having an affair."

"No way."

"You don't even know her. How can you defend her?"

"Aunt Effie says she was wonderful."

"I'm sure she was. That's no guarantee she didn't have flaws. None of us is free of sin."

"Sorry," Becky said. "Go on. What else?"

"Years went by without a clue. Then, a month or so ago, your father received an anonymous telephone call. His caller ID let him trace it to a booth in front of the grocery store, right here in Serenity."

"That was me."

"We figured that out."

"We? You mean you and Fred?"

Logan took a deep breath and tightened his grip on her slim waist. "No," he said, "me and Dan Keringhoven. I came here because he sent me. I work for him."

* * *

It took a few seconds for Logan's words to register. When they did, she tried to twist away. He held fast.

"Let me go!"

"Not till you calm down."

"Calm down? You're crazy if you think I'm going to stay here with you." She gritted her teeth and pushed against his chest. Anger surged. It blotted out everything else.

"I'm still on your side," he vowed.

"Oh, sure. Tell me another lie. You might as well. Everybody else does." She was disgusted with the emotional quaver in her voice. "I thought I knew you."

"You do know me."

The urge to yell at him was strong. "No, I don't. I thought Effie was the only one who was pretending. You're worse. At least she did it for me. You did it for the man who killed my mother."

A slight slacking of Logan's grip was all she needed to wrench free. Whirling, she ran.

"Don't condemn him till you've heard all the facts," he called after her.

"I've heard plenty," Becky shouted back.

Logan stopped in the hallway and watched her straight-arm the outer door, letting it slam behind her.

His hands fisted. So much for the subtle approach. Chances were she'd never trust him again. He didn't blame her. If he'd been in Becky's shoes, he doubted he'd have handled everything half as well, although why she didn't want to seek out her father and be certain of the facts was perplexing.

Logan had always wished he'd known his own dad better. A little boy's dreams and faded memories were a poor substitute for a real father. Good men like Fred had helped some, of course, but there was still a hollow place in his heart that even his faith hadn't fully filled. He supposed that was why he was having so much trouble understanding Becky's reluctance to come face-to-face with her father, even if the man was as despicable as Effie had claimed.

Picking up his cell phone, Logan contacted his office. "Sandra? It's me. Any more problems with Keringhoven?"

"None. He's been good as gold since you talked to him. Very polite."

"Glad to hear it. Anything else?"

"Not to speak of. I knew you didn't want him to have your private number but he was really insistent, so I gave him the number of the church. I hope that was okay."

Logan huffed. "It may explain a few things."

"Uh-oh. I goofed, huh?"

"It's nothing that can't be handled on this end," Logan said. "Just don't let clients scare you into being too helpful again, okay?"

"Okay. Sorry. Do you have any messages for Mr. K.?"

"None I can't deliver in person."

"You sound upset."

That brought a wry twist to Logan's smile. "Not half as upset as I'm going to be if I find out he hasn't kept his promise to leave this case to me."

Becky was driving too fast. She knew it. She didn't care. Right now, pointing her car down the highway and going as far as she could before she ran out of gas sounded like a great idea. If she hadn't had Aunt Effie to consider, she might have actually done it.

That train of thought made her grit her teeth. *Aunt Effie*. The one person she'd been positive she could rely on had turned out to be the biggest liar of all. Now that the truth had come out, Becky had to wonder what else was hidden in her past. How many other nasty surprises were waiting to be uncovered? Tales of runaway princesses weren't at all outlandish compared to the real facts, were they?

And what about Logan? He'd admitted coming to Serenity to search for her so there was no telling what else he was hiding. She was already blinking back tears of regret and betrayal when her thoughts progressed to Brother Fred.

Her heart leaped, lodged in her throat like bitter gall. *Fred had had to know!* He was the one who had vouched for Logan and included him in their office staff from the start. Fred was in on the subterfuge, too! There wasn't one person left she could count on. Not *one.*

Fighting tears and blurred vision, she slowed and eased her car to the right, thankful that particular stretch of highway had recently been widened. Swiping angrily at her damp cheeks she rued the day she'd opened her heart to *any* of them. Nobody could be trusted. *Nobody.*

God can, her heart told her.

"But what about those *people?*" Becky murmured. "I loved them. All of them, even Logan, and look what they did."

What have they done besides love you in return?

Becky was sobbing. "They lied to me."

She used the back of her hand to wipe her eyes. The tears flowed so freely it was a losing battle. Aware that she had no business driving when she was posing a hazard to others as well as herself, she started to pull to the side of the road.

A car had been passing on her left. It, too, slowed.

Becky barely glanced at it through her veil of sadness until it began to match her pace. Then, she blinked and stared. The car was black. Clean. And the same men who had chased her before were looking straight at her!

Overwrought, she sped up. So did they. Her foot pressed harder on the gas pedal. Who were they? Friends of Logan, maybe? It was possible. If he'd lied about other things, why not assume he'd lied about those men, too? When he'd claimed to be chasing them off he could have been meeting and exchanging information instead. What a horrible possibility!

And what about all those mysterious phone calls he'd made? No wonder he'd been so secretive. He'd been plotting against her all along. And she'd believed him. That was what hurt the most. She'd given him her total trust and he'd played her for a fool. How could she have been so stupidly blind?

Fresh tears blurred her already hampered sight. She wanted to hate them all, Logan and Fred and even Effie, but she couldn't seem to do it. All she felt was used up, abandoned and alone.

There was no way to express the absolute emptiness in her heart. All she had left was tears—and plenty of them.

Angry at herself as much as anyone, she rubbed

her eyes roughly and sniffled. The community park was to her right. If she stayed on this road she'd soon be out of town and thus more vulnerable to whoever was tracking her. *Nobody* was going to get the best of her. Not while she still had breath in her body and a brain she could use to think.

One thing was certain. She wasn't going to keep running blindly to who-knows-where. No matter how many people disappointed her, they weren't going to drive her out of town or make her decide to disappear the way Effie had. Serenity was her home. She belonged there. If anybody was leaving, it was going to be Logan Malloy—and he could take the fancy suits in the black car with him.

She checked the side mirror. The other car was still following, though not as closely as it had been. That gave her the room she figured she needed.

Coming up on a barely visible crossroad, Becky suddenly hit the brakes and whipped her steering wheel hard to the right.

Her car went into a skid. The rear slid around and fishtailed, then straightened out. She thought she'd made it. Then disaster struck. Meaning to accelerate coming out of the sharp turn, she accidentally hit the brakes.

That was the last straw. Gravity and centrifugal

force took control. Her body strained against the seat belt. The countryside seemed to be spinning and tumbling until she couldn't tell what she was seeing. All she could do was grit her teeth, hang on and ride it out.

Her tires bounced over the mounded shoulder of the highway. Briefly airborne, she hit the ground and started to skim down the grassy embankment.

That was enough to bring on an instinctive, "Father, help! Don't let me roll over," which sounded a little informal, but seemed to suffice.

The last thing she saw through the windshield was the rough bark of an oak.

Everything went white for a split second.

Then all was black.

Logan heard sirens. Normally, he wouldn't have paid much attention but since he still had Becky on his mind, the wail of the passing fire engine spurred him to action.

Running for his car, he slid behind the wheel and was on his way in seconds. No matter how many times he insisted he was being foolish, he couldn't convince himself to disregard the urge to investigate. Chances were slim that Becky was the cause of the alarm, yet he had to see for himself, had to know she was all right. And if there was a chance to minister to whoever was injured, he belonged there for that reason, too.

Such a spiritual conclusion took him by surprise. Apparently Fred had been right. There was a part of Logan Malloy that missed the ministry; missed being able to help troubled souls find their way.

"Starting with myself," he admitted cynically.

The traffic light was green and he sailed through. A fire truck up ahead was rounding a bend. Logan accelerated enough to keep the flashing red lights in sight. With no smoke in the air he had to assume the volunteer crew was on its way to an accident. He didn't want to hamper their rescue efforts or cause further problems. However, now that he'd made up his mind to help he wasn't about to let them get away, either.

Traffic was slowing. Some drivers were turning off on side streets rather than wait for the upcoming snarl to be cleared. If his memory served, there would be a widening of the highway soon, right about where the Serenity Park began. If the accident scene was near that place, he could leave his car on the park grounds. If not, he'd find a driveway or some other safe place to stop.

An ambulance appeared in his rearview mirror. Logan pulled to the side of the road to let it pass. Just ahead of him the ambulance started to slow. Looked like this was the place. He decided to leave his car right where it sat and go the rest of the way on foot.

In less than a hundred yards, a man in a tan sheriff's department uniform signaled to him and shouted, "Over here!"

Logan recognized the deputy he'd met the night he'd been mistaken for a burglar, so he knew he wasn't going to have to explain his presence or provide identification in order to offer assistance. There were some advantages to living in a small town, weren't there?

"Nathan, isn't it?" Logan asked, extending his hand.

The other man ignored his greeting, grabbed his arm, and pulled him along, instead. "Boy, am I glad to see you, Brother Malloy. The medics can't do a thing with her. Maybe she'll listen to you."

"She?" Logan's heart was in his throat. Was Becky the victim after all?

Sliding down the steep incline behind the deputy, Logan fought to keep his balance while he scanned the scene below. A car was bunched up against an enormous oak at the base of the hill. It was the only tree for hundreds of feet. If the driver had aimed for it she couldn't have hit it any squarer or done more damage.

The color of the car was the same as Becky's. That was where the similarity ended. This vehicle was so bent up, folded over and buried in the long grass it was impossible to tell its make and model. The expression on the young deputy's face, however, explained plenty.

So did the loud, familiar, "No!" coming from the gaping door on the driver's side.

Logan skidded to a stop just short of a collision with the mangled car. He leaped around the rear bumper and shouted, "Becky!" as he dropped to one knee beside her.

She reached for him and wrapped her arms around his neck as if he were heaven-sent, then quickly let go and recoiled. "Leave me alone. I never want to see you again."

"No way, lady. I'm not going anywhere until you get medical treatment."

"Why should you care? I'm just another job to you. One more case to solve. Well, you've solved it, so scram."

"You can yell at me all day and it's not going to make any difference. If you want to get rid of me, you're going to have to let the medics put you in the ambulance."

"Fine," Becky said, grimacing. "Call off your goons and I'll cooperate."

Logan's spine stiffened. His jaw muscles clenched. He scowled. "What goons?"

"The ones in the black car. Remember? You pretended to chase them away the last time."

"*They* did this to you?"

"They sure didn't help."

Logan's fists clenched as he stood and scanned the crowd that was gathering. "I don't see them. That doesn't mean they aren't here." Lowering his voice he looked directly into her puffy, red-rimmed eyes and willed her to believe him. "I came to Serenity alone," he said. "I'm still working alone. Those men aren't with me."

"Hah! You've done nothing but lie to me from the minute we met. Why in the world should I believe you?"

Before he had time to consider to the consequences or temper his answer, Logan blurted, "Because I *love* you."

Chapter Fifteen

Becky blinked. Had he really said what she thought she'd heard or was her imagination working overtime? Maybe she'd hit her head harder than she'd supposed and was hallucinating.

She licked her bruised upper lip and took a moment to study Logan's expression. He seemed sincere. Did she dare believe him? Was there room in her wounded heart for that much forgiveness?

The concern she saw in Logan's eyes was touching. Still, it was much too soon to tell whether or not he was being unduly influenced by the aftermath of her accident. He also might be saying whatever he thought she wanted to hear in order to regain her confidence. She wasn't ready to let her guard down. Not yet.

"Sorry. I don't buy that," she said as one of the paramedics fastened a cervical collar around her neck to stabilize it. "Of course, you can't go by my opinion. I just drove my car into a tree." A cynical chuckle made her wince. "Ouch. That hurts."

"Then hold still and don't get hysterical," Logan said.

"Hah! I might as well laugh at myself. Everybody else is going to. I was stupid. I never should have been on the road when I was so upset."

"It's just as much my fault for letting you go," he said. "I thought it would be best to give you room to think things through on your own. I was wrong."

"No, you weren't. I did need time by myself. I just chose the wrong way to go about it."

"That's for sure."

"You don't have to rub it in."

"Sorry."

"Me, too." She let out a shallow sigh. "I don't recommend this method of dealing with problems. It's too hard on the machinery."

"It's plenty hard on your friends, too," Logan said. "Good thing the airbag deployed or…" He cleared his throat and looked away. "Want me to ride shotgun on the way to the hospital?"

"That's not necessary." Her voice sounded harsh

in spite of her burning desire to keep him near. "I'll be fine."

"Like you were fine a few minutes ago?" he snapped back.

"I thought you weren't going to rub it in."

"Just looking for some way to help."

"Tell you what you can do. Make sure Aunt Effie has a ride to the hospital. I don't want her to think she has to steal another car to get there."

It tore Logan up to see Becky wince and bite her lip when they transferred her from the stretcher to the gurney. As soon as he could take Effie safely to the hospital and make sure Becky was going to be all right, he intended to find out if she'd simply had an accident or had been forced off the road. If it was the latter, heads were going to roll.

It wasn't a very forgiving attitude, though it did prove he was human. Even the most spiritual men had weaknesses. Rebecca Tate was one of his. A big one. Besides, it was a husband's duty to protect his wife.

That brought Logan up short. *Whoa.* First he'd admitted he loved her and now he was thinking about marriage? How dumb could he get? After all that had transpired he'd be lucky if Becky didn't tell him to get lost for good. Asking her to be his wife was out of the question. She'd never be happy in the city—or married to a detective whose life could be in danger every time he stepped out the door.

He did love her. Immeasurably. And because of that he wanted the best for her. Unfortunately, that didn't include him. What Becky needed was a gentle soul, a man like Brother Fred had been in his younger days, someone who lived his sermons every day.

It had tied his gut in a knot when he'd first caught sight of the collision. He felt even worse now. Becky was beginning to tremble due to shock. One of the attendants covered her with a gray blanket while the other secured the ambulance door, shutting him out.

Logan was instantly bereft. If parting from her temporarily was tearing him apart like this, what was it going to do to him when he had to bid her a final goodbye?

He couldn't imagine that kind of agony.

There was no answer at Effie's when Logan tried to telephone with news of the accident. He was trying to decide where to look next when he spotted Effie and Brother Fred driving by.

Logan caught up to them in the hospital parking lot and followed them inside while they checked with a nurse and were told they'd have to wait for news of Becky's condition.

Effie seemed less befuddled than Fred, at least for the moment, although she did allow Logan to put his arm around her shoulders when he greeted them both.

"How is she? Do you know?" Fred's voice cracked. "They won't tell us a thing."

"A little sore but probably fine," Logan said. "She was awake and talking to me when I got to the accident scene. We'll know more once a doctor has looked her over."

Effie's "Praise the Lord" sounded totally appropriate. Logan smiled at her. "My sentiments exactly, ma'am."

The old woman's eyebrows arched. "You didn't have nothin' to do with this, did you?"

"In a way. I said something that upset her," Logan admitted, "but I didn't cause the accident. Becky isn't sure what happened. I'm hoping she'll remember more later."

"What was it you said to her?"

Logan considered being evasive, then decided against prolonging the inevitable. Once the elderly woman found out who and what he was, he knew she'd feel the same aversion Becky had. This was a no-win situation. Nothing he said or did was going to change the facts or make him good enough for Becky. A biblical leper would have had a better chance of being accepted by her friends and family than he did.

Looking to Fred for moral support, Logan said, "I told her I was a private detective. I came to Serenity looking for her. And for you, Miss Effie." He lowered his voice. "I'm sorry."

"*You're* sorry?" She yanked free of Fred's grasp and began to back away, looking from one man to the other as if struggling to decide which of them was worse.

She settled on Fred. "I trusted you. I told you everything. How could you let me ramble on and on like that when you *knew?*"

"I never believed you were guilty of a crime," he told her, his hands outstretched pleadingly. "I still don't. I don't care what the law says, I know you acted purely out of love." He took a step closer.

"Stay away from me," she screeched. "Both of you."

Logan intervened. "Fred never told me anything you shared with him in private. He didn't have to. Becky's looks and age provided enough evidence."

"How did you find us?"

"Through an anonymous phone call Becky placed herself," Logan said. "Once she did that, it was only a matter of time till somebody figured it out and came after you."

Effie faltered, swayed.

Fred was instantly at her side, guiding her into a chair and taking the one next to her. "I didn't betray you," he said. "When Logan explained what was going on, I decided it would be best if he took charge of the situation instead of leaving it to people we didn't know. I wanted to be sure it was handled fairly."

"Nothing's fair," she wailed. "A man can abuse his wife, kill her and go free. I saved her baby and *I'm* going to be sent to jail." She looked to Fred. "I'm supposed to be forgiven. How can God let this happen?"

He patted her frail hands. "Being forgiven doesn't mean we don't have to bear the consequences of our mistakes."

"I know, but…"

When Fred put his arm around her shoulders and drew her closer, she let him. "I'll stand by you no matter what," he vowed. "We'll make it. Together. You'll see. Now that I'm retiring, you won't have any more excuses to send me packing. Face it. You're stuck with me, old girl."

Effie sniffled and took an ineffectual poke at him. "Old girl, my eye. I'm younger than you are."

"And twice as feisty," he said.

Logan was so engrossed by the tender, playful scene, the doctor's arrival took him by surprise.

"Becky's going to be fine," the white-coated man said, addressing everyone. "I don't foresee any problems. I'd like to keep her here for another hour or so though, just for observation. She should be able to go home soon."

Effie pushed forward. "I want to see her."

The doctor stepped up to block her path. "I'm sorry. She says she doesn't want to talk to anybody right now."

Placing a steadying hand on the older woman's shoulder, Logan assured her, "She's just upset. She'll get over it. She asked me to be sure you got here safely so I know she cares. I'll go tell her you're waiting."

It looked as if Effie was going to argue until Fred intervened. "Let him do it. If Becky's going to pitch a fit at any of us, I'd rather it be Logan, wouldn't you?"

"Well, since you put it that way," Effie answered.

Logan rolled his eyes. "Thanks, Brother Fred. I'll do a favor for you, sometime."

"You know what favor I want," Fred said, hugging Effie to his side.

With that plea echoing in his heart, Logan entered the cramped examination cubicle. Becky was lying on a table with her head and shoulders slightly elevated and a blanket tucked around her. Her hair was mussed, her face was smudged and her upper lip was slightly puffy. He'd never seen her look more disheveled—or more beautiful.

Approaching, Logan noted her grumpy expression. During the time they'd been apart she apparently hadn't changed her mind about him. That was undoubtedly for the best but it wasn't easy to take.

"Go away," she said, scowling.

Instead of bowing to her wishes, Logan took her hand. Her fingers were icy. He cupped them with his to try to warm them. "How are you feeling? The doctor says you're in pretty good shape."

The touch of his warm hands, the tender look in his eyes and his mellow voice melted her reserve enough to keep her from pulling away.

"I have a cracked rib, a bruised shoulder and a fat lip, which I could have told him without X-rays. Other than that, I'm in great shape. A lot better than my poor car."

"It's just metal."

"Easy for you to say. I finished paying off the loan last month. That pile of junk is all mine."

"It can be replaced. You can't."

"Humph." She was still cynical and self-derisive. "I'm definitely one of a kind, that's for sure, even if I'm not sure who I really am."

"It's who you are inside that counts." Logan

glanced in the direction of the waiting room. "Effie and Fred are waiting to see you."

"I don't think I'm ready to talk to them. Not till I get some straight answers." She was gazing deeply, pleadingly, into Logan's eyes.

"I'll tell you whatever I can," he said.

"How about starting with my real name?"

"Okay. All your birth certificate says is baby girl Keringhoven. Because you were born in December, your parents were still arguing over whether to choose Carole, Noel or Holly when you left the hospital. Dan says he just called you sweetheart."

"Terrific. How old was I when Effie ran off with me?"

"Less than a month."

"That young?" Her fingers tightened on Logan's.

"Yes. Your mother had apparently made her escape plans long before she delivered you. That was one of the things that caught your father off guard. At first, he thought her emotional problems were caused by postpartum depression. It was only later that he found out what was really going on."

"You're sure she was cheating on him?"

"As sure as anyone can be after the fact."

"Did my father really abuse her, like Aunt Effie thinks he did?"

"I doubt it," Logan said with a thoughtful shake

of his head. "I've met the man. He can be stubborn and unreasonable but I don't think he's violent."

"What about my brother?"

Logan smiled. "Ah, now we're getting to the best part. Cody's been making his living guiding white-water raft trips. A real outdoor type guy. You'll like him."

"Is there a family resemblance?"

"Well, he's taller and has a lot bigger muscles," Logan said with a wry chuckle. "Your eyes and hair are about the same color as his, though. You may want to do DNA testing just to be sure. As far as I'm concerned, you're definitely his missing sister."

"What will happen to Aunt Effie? Are you going to turn her in?"

"No. When I make my report to your father I'll try to influence him in her favor. And Fred's definitely in her corner. As a matter of fact, I think he asked her to marry him a few minutes ago."

"What?" Forgetting her soreness she sat bolt upright. "Are you sure?"

"Well, it sounded like a proposal to me."

"What did she say?"

Logan shrugged. "I don't know."

"Isn't that just like a man!" Becky threw off the blanket and swung her legs over the side of the narrow bunk.

"Whoa. The doctor didn't say you could get up yet."

"I don't care. Either you go get Aunt Effie and Brother Fred or I will."

"I thought you didn't want to see either of them."

Becky made a silly, cynical face. "I didn't. I should be furious—with all of you. But I'm so glad to be alive after the crash I can't seem to stay mad. Guess that makes me the biggest fool of all."

"Or the most loving," Logan told her with a smile of admiration. "You're quite a lady, Miss Rebecca."

"Either can the Southern charm and fetch me Effie or get out of my way," Becky insisted, attempting to stand.

Logan intervened by gently placing his hands on her shoulders. "Simmer down. I'll go." He hesitated long enough to add, "And speaking of going, I'll be heading back up north soon."

"When?"

"Probably in the next day or so. Don't worry. I won't leave till I've found out who's been following you and taken care of them."

"They really weren't working with you?"

"No. I didn't lie to you, Becky."

Releasing his hold, he backed away and headed for the door. That wasn't the only time he'd told her the absolute truth lately. His only hope was that in the confusion after the crash she either wouldn't remember what he'd confessed or would assume she'd imagined it.

He, however, wasn't imagining a thing. He'd never forget his assignment in Serenity—or the young woman he'd fallen head over heels in love with in spite of himself.

Chapter Sixteen

A tearful Effie rushed into the room and right into Becky's arms. Logan and Brother Fred stood back and let the women embrace without interference.

Finally, Becky spoke to Effie. "All right. What have you been up to while I was stuck in here? What's this I hear about marriage plans?"

"Fred was just jabbering. He knows it would never work. What kind of a wife would I make if I was stuck in jail?"

"Maybe you won't have to go to jail." She looked pleadingly at Logan. "Brother Malloy says he'll have a word with my—my father, on your behalf."

"Won't do no good," the older woman said flatly. "My goose is cooked for sure."

"Not if Logan can make him see the truth."

Approaching footsteps drew everyone's attention to the doorway, where a middle-aged man had appeared. He glowered at Logan. "I'm looking forward to hearing that."

Effie squealed and tried to hide behind Fred, setting Becky on edge. When Logan once again placed himself between her and perceived danger, the way he had when they'd been looking for the prowler at church, she didn't object.

"I think some introductions are in order," Logan said formally. "Mr. Keringhoven, I'd like you to meet your daughter, Rebecca. You already know me and I think you recognize Miss Effie. The other gentleman is Brother Fred Fleming."

Peeking past Logan, Becky sized up the man who was supposedly her father. In spite of his wrinkled forehead, thick, gray eyebrows and thinning hair, he didn't look menacing. Certainly not dangerous. In fact, judging by the tears glistening in his eyes, he was anything but irate.

When she stood and nudged Logan aside, he steadied her with an arm around her shoulders.

"I never thought I'd see my girl again," the man whispered. "Why didn't you tell me how beautiful she was? She looks just like her mother."

"I thought so, too," Logan said. "That was one of the things that helped convince me."

Effie was quivering but far from silent. "Don't you listen to that man. He's the devil himself!"

"Why?" Dan asked, finally turning his attention to his accuser. "How could you do this to me? I treated you like a member of the family. Why did you steal my baby?"

"Flo's baby, you mean," Effie answered. "You didn't deserve to have her. Not after the way you acted."

Logan watched their exchange with interest. Clearly, the man was confounded by her accusations rather than being defensive.

Speaking quietly so Effie would have to hush to hear him, Logan said, "Suppose Florence had a different motive for wanting to leave. I know it was a long time ago but try to remember. Think, Miss Effie. Was there something else going on in your friend's life back then? Something she might have been embarrassed to tell you?"

"No. Of course not. She…"

Waiting, Logan saw doubt cross her face, saw her blink rapidly as she began to consider his question.

"Why would she lie to me?" Effie asked in a near whisper.

"To keep her children?"

"She didn't have to run away to do that."

"Didn't she? If she'd divorced my client and gone

to another man, especially one she'd been having an affair with, she might have lost custody on moral grounds. By getting you to help, she not only covered her tracks, she set you up to watch the kids while she continued to have her fun. If she hadn't had that fatal accident, her plan would have succeeded."

The older woman's eyes widened. "It can't be."

"I never laid a hand on my wife," Keringhoven vowed. "Never. Not even when she laughed in my face and taunted me with her affairs. I loved her too much."

Behind him, the outer door banged. In seconds, a younger, taller version of Becky's Nordic-looking father poked his head in the room and said, "Sorry it took me so long to park the car, Dad. I had trouble finding an empty spot."

Effie gasped, made a grab for Brother Fred's arm, and wilted like a plucked daisy on a hot summer day.

Fred had refused to leave Effie's side, even after she was admitted to the hospital for observation. Finally, her doctor had stopped trying to convince him to go home and had had a reclining chair brought in so he could doze nearby in comfort.

It had taken Logan hours to convince Becky that she'd be foolish to stay, too. He knew it was more her pain than his persuasiveness that had pushed her to let him drive her home. That was okay. Anything was fine with him as long as it was best for Becky.

She'd laid her head back and closed her eyes as soon as he'd helped her into the car. Logan had decided not to insist she use the seat belt. The one in her car had probably saved her from more serious injury but it had also caused her cracked rib and a very sore left shoulder. All in all, it seemed like a pretty fair trade, considering how badly she could have been hurt.

That terrible thought tied his gut in another knot and made his palms clammy. Every instinct told him to take her in his arms and tell her he loved her, over and over again. The only thing stopping him was the realization of how unfair it would be, especially to her.

Tenderly, he asked, "Are you riding okay?"

"Fine." There was a slight lift to the corners of her mouth. Her eyes opened lazily. "How slow are you driving, anyway?"

"I didn't want to jostle you."

"I think a little faster would be all right. It would be nice to get home sometime today."

"I see you haven't lost your sense of humor."

"Guess not. So, tell me more about my family. How soon can I see them again?" Her blue eyes widened. "You didn't send them away, did you?"

"No." Logan gave her a smile of encouragement. "After Effie fainted, your dad thought it best to make himself scarce. He hasn't gone far. Neither has Cody."

"A brother," Becky murmured, "I have a real brother. I've always wanted one."

"And a father?" Logan asked.

"I don't know about that part. It's a lot to get used to all at once."

"True enough. I'm not sure how I'd react if my father popped back into my life. Probably not as well as you have."

"My situation is different. In a way, my father and I were both victims."

"If I can make him realize that, too, it should make things easier for everyone."

Becky's brow furrowed. "What's next for you?"

"File my final report and go back to Chicago, I guess. My work here is done."

"Whoa. What about the men in the black car?"

"I'm working on that."

"I certainly hope so." Laying her head back once again she started to take a deep breath. Pain cut it short. "Do you have any leads?"

"Not that I'm ready to share."

She gave him a disgusted look. "Here we go again, huh? Guess I'll never learn."

"What's that supposed to mean?"

"Nothing," she said wearily. "I'm just overtired. Forget it."

Weariness of her soul caused her to hold her tongue. She was tired, all right. Tired of being sheltered. Tired of being protected. Just because someone else had made a decision, supposedly in her best interests, didn't mean it was right.

She sighed. Someday, hopefully, the people she loved were going to wake up and realize she needed the truth a lot more than she needed to be coddled.

Except for hearing the truth about Logan's plans, she added. She'd *never* be ready to hear he was leaving for good. Never.

The old house seemed empty without Effie. Normal creaks and groans stood out the way the noise of the prowler had at church. If Becky hadn't been suffering the aftereffects of the accident and dulled senses due to the mild painkiller the doctor had prescribed, she would have been too fidgety to doze. As it was, however, she soon fell asleep propped on pillows piled at one end of the living room sofa.

Night came. She awoke to a stab of pain when she tried to turn over. Pressing her hands tightly against her side she waited for the ache to go away. It merely eased.

Moving with care, she sat up. Obviously the pain medication had worn off and it was time to take more, so where had she left her purse? Come to think of it, what was she doing in the living room?

Vague memories of Logan dropping her off drifted through her muzzy mind. She'd meant to go to bed after sending him away. Apparently, she'd been so worn out she hadn't gotten any farther than the comfort of the couch.

She was about to get to her feet and go searching for the purse containing her prescription when she thought she heard a muffled sound at the rear of the house.

"Aunt Effie?" she called.

Wait a minute. Effie wasn't there. No one else was. So what was she hearing?

A stab of pain shot through her as she stood. Clutching her ribs, she paused to catch her breath. This was one time she wished she had bought Effie a dog—only not a lap dog. What they needed was a big, protective German shepherd with an attitude, preferably in her favor.

Switching on the lamp and reaching for the telephone on the end table, she put the receiver to her ear. Dialing 911 wasn't going to help this time. The line was dead!

Frantic, she realized her cell phone was her only

remaining connection to the world outside—and it was in the purse she'd misplaced.

So now what? Flee? How far would she get when the slightest move hurt so much it took her breath away?

Hide? That was out of the question, too. Any closet or cupboard that had had a bit of room was stuffed with Effie's hobby supplies, Christmas decorations and the spare clothing they'd been saving to give to a homeless shelter.

Becky gritted her teeth. *Stand and fight? How?* Lifting their biggest iron frying pan had taken two hands before she'd cracked a rib. Now, it would be impossible.

China crashed to the floor in the kitchen. Someone groaned.

Run! her most basic instinct shouted.

No. Somebody might need help.

"Yeah, somebody like me," she muttered.

Disgusted with herself for being so self-centered, Becky scooped up one of the throw pillows and hugged it to her side. It cushioned her movement enough to allow her to tiptoe silently to the kitchen and peek in.

The beam of a flashlight was sweeping the room. The place was in shambles. She ducked back too late when the light swung her way. She'd been seen!

"Wait!" a hushed voice ordered.

Becky didn't listen. Bent on escape, she zigzagged past the living room furniture and burst out the front door, no longer mindful of her injuries.

She was almost to the base of the porch steps when a shadow loomed beside her. One strong arm grabbed and held her while a hand muffled her scream.

Though the hand was clad in a leather glove she tried to bite it. The nip was enough to loosen the man's grip. Becky tossed her head and used his momentary lapse to let out a piercing screech followed by "Help!"

Suddenly, she was loose! Falling to her knees on the dewy lawn she crawled away, fully expecting to be caught and assaulted again. Instead, she was able to reach the base of the flower bed and tuck herself beneath the heavy branches of a cascading forsythia, long past its yellow bloom.

The moon slipped from behind a drifting cloud, partially lighting the scene. Two large figures in dark clothes were struggling at the foot of the porch steps. At first, she wondered if the men who had followed her might be the ones fighting. Logic refuted that possibility.

She edged farther into the shadows and waited, hoping and praying the victor would be someone who was on her side. Someone like Logan Malloy. She'd give anything to see him drive up about now, even if she was still distressed over his announcement that he was leaving Serenity for good.

One of the men drew back and landed a punch that rocked his opponent. The other man fell. Lay still. Becky held her breath. There was something familiar about the way the victor moved. The set of his shoulders reminded her of Logan. So did the way he ran his fingers through his tousled hair to comb it back.

She was already certain she wasn't imagining things when he said, "Rebecca? Where are you? Are you all right?"

"Yes." It was a verbal sigh. "I'm here."

He dropped to his knees in front of her.

She came to him without hesitation and slipped her arms around his waist. Laying her cheek on his chest she listened to his racing heart and felt him gently caressing her hair.

"I was afraid I'd lost you," Logan said breathlessly.

"Was that you in the kitchen?"

"Yes. I took care of one of them in there. You ran off before I could warn you. I knew the other one had to be close by. I just couldn't be in two places at once."

"Seems to me you did a pretty fair job of it."

"Not good enough." He held her away long enough to give her a relieved look. "Did you call the police?"

"No. The line was dead and I couldn't find my cell phone. I don't know what happened to my purse after the accident. I thought I had it at the hospital."

"You did. You left it in my car when I drove you home." Logan got to his feet and took her hands to help her up. "I was parked down the block, watching your place, when I noticed the purse and remembered your pain medication was in it. I was bringing it to you when I caught those guys breaking in. I don't know how they got past me."

She saw him press his lips into a thin line. His jaw muscles clenched. She caressed his cheek, mindless of the beard stubble. "It's okay. I got what I wanted."

"What was that?"

"You," she said softly. Her lips parted. Her hand slipped around the back of Logan's neck and she urged him closer. She knew she wasn't being over-confident. Not this time. She might not have had much experience with men but she could tell enough to know that Logan wanted to kiss her as much as she wanted to kiss him. She was right.

His mouth barely brushed hers, then lingered. When he finally leaned away he was clearly moved. "I don't want to hurt you," he whispered.

Becky knew he was referring to her injured lips but her heart gave his words deeper meaning. If something didn't happen to change his mind about leaving town he *was* going to hurt her. Terribly. She just didn't know how to keep that from happening—or if she should even try.

Rather than dwell on such a depressing scenario she concentrated on imagining a humorous side to her dilemma. She wasn't desperate enough to throw herself bodily in front of his car to stop him from going away, so that idea was no good. And she had too much pride to cling to him and beg him to stay.

There were only two things she was ready and willing to do; pray with every ounce of faith she could muster, and kiss him again, preferably more than once.

Praying wasn't going to be difficult.

Giving Logan a few tender kisses, then calling a halt and distancing herself from him was going to be much, much harder.

Chapter Seventeen

They'd used Logan's cell phone to summon the police. Naturally, all the commotion had brought the neighbors out in droves, giving Becky and Logan no more private time.

It was the next morning before she saw him again. Her first thought was that he must have dropped by her house to bid her a final goodbye. She preempted the strike with a cheerful, "Hello."

"Hi. How are you feeling this morning?"

"Like somebody threw me off the porch." She laughed when she saw he was taking her too seriously. "I'm fine. Fred called."

"Did you tell him what happened last night?"

"Yes. Effie wanted to come straight home when she heard about it. I convinced her to stay in the hospital till her doctor runs those tests he had planned."

"Good. I stopped by to tell you our mystery is solved. Your visitors last night were private investigators."

She instinctively wrapped her arms around her waist and held tight. "Who hired them?"

"Your father."

"What?"

"It's not as bad as it sounds. Dan got impatient. I didn't move fast enough to suit him so he brought in another firm. They weren't supposed to do anything but keep an eye on you."

Becky huffed. "I'd hate to see what they'd do if they were told to get rough." Noticing that Logan was staring at the way she was favoring her sore side, she added, "I'm okay. Honest. You don't need to go knock them in the head again."

"They're fortunate that's all I did."

While he was in such a protective mood she decided to forge ahead. "I'm glad you dropped by. I need to talk to you. Fred wants you to preach this coming Sunday."

"Why? What's wrong with him?"

"Nothing. He doesn't plan to come back to work until Effie's out of the hospital so he wants you to take over his duties, including worship services."

"What put that idiotic notion into his head? Fred knows better than to ask me to preach. I don't belong in a pulpit. I realized that a long time ago."

Becky was smiling wryly in spite of her tender upper lip. "Did you? Well, I guess we'll see, won't we?"

"No way. Call somebody else."

"I suppose I could. If I was of a mind to," she drawled. "But I've been injured, you know. I doubt I'll be well enough to go to the office for quite some time. Sorry."

He grimaced. "I'm getting the idea Fred's not the one who's really behind this sudden request to hear me make a fool of myself in front of the whole congregation."

"You'll do fine."

"That's a matter of opinion."

Becky nodded sagely. "Exactly."

Late that afternoon, Logan once again appeared at Becky's door. He wasn't smiling. Nevertheless, she greeted him pleasantly. "Hi, again. Trouble at work? You could have phoned if you had questions."

"That's not why I'm here."

His demeanor was sobering. Her smile waned. "Okay. Are you going to tell me what's wrong or do I have to guess?"

"Dan wants a meeting."

"When?"

"Now. I'll drive you."

"Just like that? No *please* or anything?"

Logan nodded. "I tried to convince him it would be better to wait."

"Well?"

"He blew up at me and started yelling. I backed off so he'd calm down. He says he's made up his mind and wants to get everything settled before he goes back to Chicago."

"What is it with you people?" Becky complained. "Seems like you can't wait to get out of Serenity. Is it *that* bad here? Have we made you feel unwelcome or something?"

"Not at all," Logan said. He checked his watch. "Grab your purse and let's go. We don't want to be late."

"Of course not." Her voice was tinged with sarcasm. "So, where is this important meeting, anyway?"

She almost gasped when Logan said, "In Effie's hospital room. Everybody's going to be there."

Becky thought she was doing well to even speak, let alone ask pertinent questions during the short drive to the hospital. Trouble was, Logan refused to give her straight answers. His reticence was more than worrying. It was frightening.

She tried again as they left the car. "You must have some idea what he's planning."

"Not much."

"Then at least tell me what you think. Is he going to have Aunt Effie arrested?"

"I honestly don't know."

"What about Brother Fred? Will he be in trouble, too? I mean, if the authorities thought he'd been protecting her all these years, wouldn't he be considered guilty of aiding and abetting?"

"Probably. If that happens, we can swear under oath that he was as much in the dark as you were."

"Will they believe us?"

"I hope so." Logan held the door for her, then followed her onto the elevator and pushed the button for the second floor. "Unfortunately, it's been my experience that our justice system can be fallible. Are you ready for a long, hard fight?"

"If it comes to that," Becky answered. "I won't let anything bad happen to Aunt Effie if there's any way to prevent it. She doesn't deserve to go to prison."

"I'm glad to hear you're still calling her your aunt. I was worried about your relationship."

Becky managed a slight smile. "So was I. After

the initial shock wore off, I realized how much she must have loved me, and my mother, to have done what she did for us. I'm just sorry everything turned out so badly."

The door to Effie's room stood open. Becky halted outside to gather her courage and felt the light touch of Logan's hand at the small of her back. This time, she didn't object. Considering how much she was dreading entering that room, she was more than glad she wasn't alone.

"I feel kind of like a teenager who's late getting home from a date," she told Logan. "Only this is worse. I have to face an irate father I don't even know. How can I hope to reason with him when we're strangers?"

"I'll be right here with you."

Becky made a cynical face. "Terrific. You're the one he just yelled at. He's probably even madder at you than he is at me."

"Possibly." Logan gave her a nudge.

"Don't push. I'm going."

"Yes, ma'am."

The hint of teasing in his voice helped her step forward. Curtains were drawn between Effie's bed and the door. Beneath the curtain, Becky counted three sets of men's shoes. Only one set belonged to Brother Fred.

She called out, "Aunt Effie? I'm here."

The curtain slid partway back on squeaking overhead rollers. Dan Keringhoven held it aside. He was glaring at Logan. "What took you so long?"

"You're early," Logan countered.

Cody stepped between them. "That's my fault. I don't have much patience. I figured we might as well wait here instead of pacing our rooms at the motel."

Becky greeted him with a smile and offered her hand. "Must be a family trait. I'm the same way."

Her brother shook hands warmly. "Well, at least we're seldom late."

"True." She transferred her attention to Effie and Fred. They were grasping each other's hands as if they were afraid to let go. Clearly, Effie had been crying.

"You two okay?" Becky asked.

Fred nodded, obviously desperately worried.

Struck by the unfairness of the location Dan had chosen for their meeting, Becky whirled and faced him. "Okay. I've had about enough of this. I'm not going to stand here and let you torture these poor people any more. If you have something to say to me, I'll be out in the hall."

"Wait," Dan said. "Don't go. You'll miss the best part."

"Of what?" Becky wasn't about to capitulate without good reason.

"I've consulted my lawyer in regard to this whole situation," he said.

Effie began to sob softly in the background and Becky went to her side before saying, "The only way to be fair is for you to forget everything that's happened."

"I'll never forget," Dan said with emotion. "I wouldn't want to. I loved my wife. I love my son." He hesitated. "And I want to get to know my daughter. Maybe, someday, we can build the kind of relationship we should have had in the first place."

"Not if you send Aunt Effie to prison!"

"I see that. That's why I talked to my attorney. I had already decided not to reveal any secrets or press charges but I was worried about legalities. If there is a problem, my lawyer will be ready to provide a good defense. Florence was the one who's really guilty. She set up the scheme and gave the orders. That should put Effie in the clear even if the police stir things up later."

"Really?" Becky was awed. "I don't know what to say. I thought…"

"You don't have to explain. I understand. You'd spent so many years hating me, you assumed I'd want revenge." He made a self-deprecating noise. "I *was* mad. Furious, as a matter of fact. Then I got to thinking about what might have happened when you were a baby. If Effie hadn't taken you away with her before Flo's crash, you could have been in that mangled car, too."

Dan paused to blow his nose. "All that was brought back to me when I heard you'd been in an accident. The similarity to your mother's death was appalling. I could have lost you all over again. I never want that to happen."

Becky was dumbfounded.

"I know we have a lot of obstacles to overcome," her father said, "but I'd like to try."

Her gaze swept around the room. Everyone was staring at her, waiting. No one moved. No one spoke.

Finally, Becky released the grin she'd been holding back and centered it on her father. "So would I," she said. "What do you say you and I go get a cup of coffee? Looks like we have a lot to talk about."

"I'd love to."

It pleased her to note how relieved Dan seemed. Whatever his reasons for offering to help Effie, the result would be for the good. That was what mattered.

"We'll have to take your car. Mine's in the shop," Becky said lightly. "Probably permanently."

"Aren't there any car dealers around here?"

"We have little used car lots all over the place. I'll be able to find something I can afford. I just haven't had time to look yet."

"I take it nobody's told you what I do for a living," Dan said.

"Sell used cars?"

"No, new ones. What's your favorite color?"

Becky pulled a silly face. "Don't tease. I might take you seriously."

"I expect you to," Dan said. "My hired idiots caused your accident so I figure I owe you a car. I have some sales brochures with me. All you have to do is take a look, pick one out, and I'll have it shipped down to you."

Her glance darted to Logan for affirmation. The look on his face was a cross between shock and amusement.

Becky's already frazzled nerves were making the whole situation seem unduly amusing. She giggled. "I thought kids were supposed to have a lot of trouble talking their parents into getting them a car. I don't know what to say. This is way too easy."

From across the room came a chorus of encouragement. Logan's "Stop arguing and take the car!" carried best.

She turned to her father with a wide grin. "I'd be

pleased to look at your brochures and choose. I'm especially fond of blue."

"Done."

Dan offered his arm and Becky took it as they left the hospital room. It seemed strange to have a father beside her, let alone such a benevolent one. She was so overwhelmed she couldn't stop grinning at him like a silly child.

Which isn't so bad, she decided easily. It looked like Dan Keringhoven had a softer side to his gruff persona after all. Given enough time, maybe they would find common ground and become like the family she'd missed.

It was certainly worth the effort to find out—and *not* just because he was giving her a new car!

Chapter Eighteen

Brother Fred had kept his promise and stayed away from the office for the remainder of the week. The only time Becky had seen him was when she'd spelled him at Effie's bedside. Effie was playing up her supposed frailty for all it was worth. Becky suspected she was relying on her hospitalization to keep from accidentally running into Dan while he was in town, even though he'd promised he wouldn't prosecute.

Part of the credit for that happy decision went to Logan. Some obviously lay with Cody, too. Thoughts of her newfound brother made her smile. He was not only polite and handsome, he radiated an aura of kindness and easygoing acceptance that was harder to see in their father. That was why, when she decided to invite both of them to church, she chose to call Cody first.

He answered his cell phone immediately. "Hello?"

"Cody? It's me, Becky."

"Hi, kiddo. What's up?"

"Actually, I was wondering if you and Dad would like to come to church with me tomorrow?"

"I would. Dad's gone."

"Gone? Where?"

"Home. He took off like a shot this morning. I know he tried to call your house before he left. I heard him."

"Oh, dear. I dropped by the hospital to see how Effie was doing. I wasn't home."

"So, how is she? Has she settled down any?"

"Yes. It's wonderful. The doctors have decided which medications will help her and she's actually making sense almost all the time now."

"That's great."

"You really mean that, don't you?" Becky was touched by her brother's sincere concern.

"Of course I do. She raised my baby sister."

"I wish we could go back," Becky said.

Cody took a moment to reply. "I don't. It was different for me, being a boy and being older when

Mom died. I'm not sure how Dad would have coped with raising a daughter, especially one who grew up to look so much like Mom. He'd have done his best, I know, but he's human. Being with Effie may have been the best place for you."

"I hadn't thought of it that way." She paused. "I wish I'd had a chance to say goodbye to him before he left."

"Chicago's not that far away. When you get your new car why don't you drive up to visit him?"

"I might," she said with a smile. "I don't know how I'd fare in heavy traffic, though." She chuckled softly. "I have enough trouble avoiding trees that jump out in front of me."

Cody had promised to meet Becky in the church parking lot. She spotted him walking toward her and mirrored his smile. "Welcome. I'm glad you could come."

"Thanks for inviting me," Cody said. "This church is a lot smaller than the one I go to at home."

"Really? Serenity Chapel has just about the biggest congregation in Fulton County, although size isn't what makes it so special."

He fell into step beside her. "I agree. That Brother Fred of yours is quite a guy. Real likeable."

"Fred's the sweetest, kindest man in the world but he's getting old, bless his heart. He's definitely earned his retirement. Getting him to take it is what's going to be hard. He hates to let go. That's one of the reasons I asked Logan to step in and preach this morning."

"Logan Malloy? The detective?"

"The same. He's actually an ordained minister."

"You're kidding! I never would have dreamed he had it in him."

Becky laughed. "You're not the only one. Logan isn't real sure, either."

The church filled up quickly. Becky wasn't at all taken aback when Carol Sue Grabowski and Trudy Lynn Brown squeezed into the pew directly behind them and tapped her on the shoulder with a cheery, "Good morning!"

Becky pivoted and smiled. "Well, what a nice surprise. I'd like you ladies to meet my brother, Cody. Cody, this is Carol Sue and Trudy. They're members of my Sunday school class." Her grin widened. "My *singles* class."

He stood briefly and acknowledged the attractive women. For his sake, Becky was thankful the service was about to begin. As usual, the members of

Miss Louella's Extraordinary Ladies Class were the first to answer a challenge. If her eligible brother didn't leave Serenity soon, as planned, he'd be the object of plenty more flattering female interest.

Becky stifled a grin. Maybe she should take lessons from those other women and try batting her eyelashes at Logan Malloy to get him to hang around. *That would be the day!*

And speaking of Logan, she hadn't seen him since they'd passed in the hall before Sunday school. That was worrisome. If he'd ducked out on her—or on Brother Fred—she was going to be very disappointed. In more ways than one.

Everyone stood for the opening hymn. Still no Logan. Becky was starting to get antsy. Where was he? Come to think of it, why hadn't he stayed out front to greet parishioners? He knew that was what Fred always did.

But Logan isn't Fred, she reminded herself soberly. No matter who took over the pastorate of Serenity Chapel, some things were bound to change. Life was like that.

Eyes widening, she realized the wisdom of what she'd just told herself. She'd been fighting against that very thing, resisting any changes to her safe little world without giving the subject conscious consideration. She'd been going about this all wrong. Getting Logan to stay in Serenity and change his lifestyle to suit her wasn't the answer. If she *really* loved him, she wouldn't care where they went or what he did for a living, as long as they were together.

And she *did* love him. That much was undeniable. Given his admission that he felt the same way about her, his plans to leave Serenity made no sense. The least he could do was stick around long enough to give their relationship a chance. That was only fair.

She was about to make a dash for the side door, hunt him down and tell him exactly that, when he appeared. Becky had never seen him look more handsome, more appealing, or more ill-at-ease. As soon as his gaze met hers, she gave him her most encouraging smile and wiggled the fingers beneath her hymnal in a surreptitious wave.

Logan reddened and looked away, giving her a glimmer of hope. Maybe he hadn't changed his mind about what he'd said at the accident scene. Her heart soared in the few moments it took for logic to intervene.

More likely, his flushed complexion was a reaction to the sight of the packed sanctuary. Even the most seasoned pastor was bound to struggle with nervousness from time to time. In Logan's case, his battle seemed to be within himself as well as with the job, so it was no wonder he looked so uncomfortable.

Loving him, she quietly bowed her head and began to pray for his success. And for his peace. Personal concerns would wait.

Logan laid his note cards on the lectern when he rose to speak. This sermon was going to be his first in a long time—and also his last. He'd agonized over what he should focus on, changing his mind again and again. Something inside him kept insisting his future was wrapped up in what he was about to say and he didn't like that feeling one bit.

Squinting against the bright lights trained on the pulpit, he stared at the congregation and quietly cleared his throat. To his chagrin, the microphone he wore was sensitive enough to pick up even that. Too bad he hadn't forced himself to eat breakfast. The way his clerical career had gone so far, this congregation was liable to hear his stomach growling loud and clear before he was through.

It's not about me, he suddenly thought. *It never*

was. That was what was so different this time! It didn't matter how he spoke or whether his delivery was as perfect and eloquent as Fred's. The message was what was important. He must have known that once, long ago. Why had he forgotten?

The note cards fluttered to the floor. Logan ignored them. His voice as strong as his conviction, he began to speak from the heart.

"I didn't come to Serenity to preach to you," he said boldly. "I came to help Brother Fred in another way. At the time, I thought my motives were pure. I meant them to be. But I was wrong. About a lot of things."

Pausing, he peered through the brightness to settle his gaze on Becky. She was giving him her rapt attention.

"I met Fred Fleming years ago, in seminary," Logan continued. "He was more than my teacher. He was my mentor. I know many of you see him as a father figure. I did, too. And a very special friend. So, when I got an opportunity to step in and help him, I jumped at it."

In the congregation, heads were nodding in agreement and appreciation.

"I thought I was doing it as a favor for Fred but I was fooling myself. You see, I'm an imposter."

A murmur of unrest started to rumble through the room. Logan held up his hands. "It's not as bad as it sounds. I was ordained a long time ago. Then life intervened and I fell away from the ministry. Or maybe I should say I turned my back on it and walked away. The bottom line is, I was making my living as a private investigator when one of my cases brought me to Fred's doorstep. I guess that was when my outlook began to shift. I'm a slow learner. It's taken me this long to realize it."

Stepping out from behind the lectern, Logan spread his hands wide, palms out. "I'm supposed to stand up here and tell you you're lost sinners in need of Christ. Well, so am I. I've been lost for a long time. God's been telling me I needed to come home and I've been doing my best to ignore Him. That's over."

His head bowed. "I'm done running, Father. If You want me back You can have me. I don't have a clue what You'd want with a guy like me but that's okay. I know You'll show me."

Stepping down off the podium and turning to face the altar, he knelt and began to pray silently.

Becky was awed. Logan's brief, poignant sermon had gone beyond her fondest hopes. He'd preached it with his own life. And judging by the stirring she heard behind her, his example of faith was already producing results.

She stood, paused, then quietly went forward to kneel beside him. Others were filing down the aisles, too; some with great joy, some with tears, some alone and some accompanied by family members.

The choir director began to sing a praise anthem. The congregation joined in.

At the altar, Becky reached out to Logan and grasped his hand. No words were necessary. Sharing that moment was enough. If she'd had her way, it would have lasted for an eternity.

"But you have to stay now," Becky argued as they locked up after the service. "Everybody wants you to."

Logan wouldn't be swayed. "It's not that simple. I have other responsibilities."

"You said you were giving your life back to God. Didn't you mean it?"

"Of course I did. But it doesn't follow that I'm supposed to immediately pack up and go become a missionary in some distant land."

She followed him up the main aisle of the sanctuary and waited while he checked the locks on the front doors. "Serenity is *not* a distant land."

"No, and I'm not a missionary. At least I don't think I am. Time will tell."

"That's it? That's all? You're just going to walk away after what you did this morning? We've never had a revival like the one you just started. Folks who hardly ever go to church were coming up to me afterward and volunteering to help with whatever we need. It's amazing."

Logan was slowly shaking his head and smiling at her. "I didn't do a thing, Becky. God did. You can have a continued revival with Brother Fred or whoever takes his place. You don't need me."

"Wrong," she said, steeling herself for the worst. "Maybe Serenity Chapel doesn't need you but *I* do." She saw his eyes begin to narrow, his jaw set.

In spite of that, she decided to forge ahead. This was not the time to give up or back down. "I may have been a little woozy after I tangled with that tree and scrunched my poor old car," she told him, "but I heard *exactly* what you said."

"Uh-oh."

"Don't try to deny it. You said you loved me." Hands fisted on her hips, she stood firm and faced him. "Well? Do you or don't you?"

One corner of Logan's mouth quirked in a suppressed smile. "We're standing inside a church. If I say, 'I do,' does that make us married?"

"If I thought it would, I'd say it, too."

"Is that what you want?" he asked softly.

She had to talk fast before she lost her nerve or leaped into Logan's arms like a lovesick teenager. "Yes."

"Well, well. And would you be willing to leave here and follow me if I decided to go be a missionary in Africa—or Chicago?"

Trembling and stepping closer, she gazed at him. "Yes. I would."

"Okay. I accept. I'll marry you."

"What?" Eyes wide, she planted her palms on his chest and gave him a push. "That's not how it's supposed to go. You're supposed to propose to *me*."

Logan grinned. *"Now* she tells me."

"Logan…" She'd started to smile at him in spite of herself.

"Oh, all right." He took her hand and dropped to one knee. "Miss Rebecca, will y'all marry up with me?"

Of all the romantic moments she'd ever imagined, none had begun to measure up to the pure delight of this one. If Logan expected her to take exception to his theatrical actions or his exaggerated southern drawl he had another think coming.

With a grin so broad her cheeks hurt, she said, "I'd be proud to."

"Even if you have to live in the big city?"

"Even there. I'll follow you anywhere."

He stood and took her in his arms. "I believe you would. So, tell me, how soon do you want to become Mrs. Logan Malloy?"

Becky rested her cheek on his chest and sighed. "I don't know. Yesterday?"

Her silly answer made him laugh and she took a moment to revel in the surge of pleasure his good humor gave her before continuing. "Actually, I was thinking of a Christmas wedding. Maybe around the time of my birthday?" She tilted her face to gaze at him. "I hope you know when that is, because I'm not real sure."

"Early December," Logan said. "And I think it's a wonderful idea. We can invite your whole family to celebrate the holidays with us."

"Effie and Fred, too," Becky added. "I just hope they're up to traveling that far in the winter."

"Far? Who said anything about going far?"

"But, I thought…"

Logan kissed her silent. "You think too much, honey. I wouldn't dream of taking you away from Serenity, except maybe on our honeymoon. We'll live here, even if I have to commute all the way to Chicago!"

"You mean that?"

"Absolutely. And if it's okay with you, I'd like to ask Fred to marry us."

Astounded, Becky nodded. If life got any better she was going to burst from trying to contain such sheer joy. Blinking back tears of happiness she whispered, "I love you, Logan."

Just before he bent to kiss her he grinned and said, "Bless your little heart. I love you, too, darlin'."

Epilogue

Becky had thought Effie and Fred might want to combine their nuptials and join her and Logan for a double wedding but the older couple had declined. They'd said they couldn't bear to spend time apart, and who could argue with that? In his first official act as the church's new pastor, Logan had performed their ceremony in front of the entire Serenity Chapel family, much to everyone's delight.

Fred had gladly come out of retirement for Becky's Christmas wedding a few months later. At that time, the chapel sanctuary had already been decorated with banks of rich red poinsettias and evergreen boughs. Those colors had set off her white gown like snow against the cedars on the Ozark hills, and the sun streaming through the stained glass windows had added a rosy glow.

Best of all, her father had agreed to give her away. Walking down the aisle on Dan Keringhoven's arm, she'd felt like all her dreams had come true. And now that the reception was over and she and Logan were finally at home, surrounded by close family and a few friends, she was sure of it.

"Aunt Effie's been cooking for days," Becky told her guests. "I'm surprised she was able to tear herself away from the stove long enough to come to the wedding this morning. I tried to help her but she said I had enough to worry about and banished me from my own kitchen."

Logan chuckled. "Probably just as well."

She made a face and took a mock swipe at him. "My cooking's not that bad. I baked the pies last night."

"After you took them out of the freezer?" her new husband asked knowingly.

That brought gales of laughter from everyone, especially Dan and Cody.

"I'm so glad you could come," Becky told them. "I've never had Christmas with anyone but Aunt Effie." She blinked rapidly to hide her overflowing emotions. "It was always wonderful, of course, but I never thought I'd have a whole family to celebrate with like this."

Logan stepped closer and put his arm around her shoulders. "There's more good news," he said. "That's why I've asked Effie and Fred to come out of the kitchen and join us for a minute."

Looking past Dan, Becky smiled at the older couple standing in the doorway. Their closeness mirrored the way Logan was hugging her and made her appreciate anew how truly blessed they all were to have each other.

Logan deferred to Becky's father. "Dan, would you like to tell them?"

The older man cleared his throat and sniffled. "I'd rather you did it."

If Logan hadn't tightened his grip on her shoulders at just the right moment, Becky might have trembled. Obviously, something important was about to be revealed.

"Okay," Logan said. "It's like this. Dan's had a team of attorneys working on the abduction case for months and they've managed to iron everything out. Effie's in the clear. For good."

Squeals of joy and applause filled the room while Fred drew his wife closer and kissed her cheek.

"The mixed-up birth certificates have been correctly filed and all criminal charges have been withdrawn," Logan continued. "Becky is—I mean, was—a Keringhoven before she became a Malloy this morning. Dan left Rebecca listed as her first name to simplify things." He grinned down at her. "We figured she was already confused enough about her identity."

Becky winked at her father. "As long as I get to belong to this crazy family, you can call me anything you want." She giggled. "Within reason."

"I think it's time to share the rest of your surprise," Logan told his new father-in-law. "I know you were going to wait till after we'd eaten and were exchanging our regular gifts but this seems like a perfect opportunity."

"I agree," Dan said. "Everybody stay right where you are. I'll be back in a jiffy."

Becky frowned. "The man already gave me a brand-new car. How in the world can he top that?"

"You'll see."

She was surprised to see Dan bearing a gift the size of a small shoebox when he returned. He handed it to her without comment so she asked, "What is it?"

"Open it," her father said hoarsely.

The faded holiday wrapping paper was so brittle it crumbled when she pulled on it. Letting the scraps fall to the floor at her feet, Becky carefully lifted the lid off the box. Her vision blurred. Inside, resting in a bed of yellowed tissue paper, was a simple baby doll dressed in pastel pink.

"I bought that for your first Christmas," Dan said, his voice breaking. "I've kept it all these years, hoping…"

"It's the best present I've ever gotten," Becky said, beaming through unshed tears. "I'll treasure it always. Thanks, Daddy."

Logan pulled her closer, lifted the doll from its nest of paper and held it up, cradled in one hand. "She has your beautiful hair and eyes. I hope our kids look just like this." He paused for a low chuckle. "Of course, they'll all have to be boys."

Becky played along by pretending to be astonished, as if they hadn't discussed eventually starting a family. "All? How many do you want?"

"Oh, no more than five or six," he joked. "If we decide to form our own little league team we can always wait till Cody gets married and provides us with a few cousins."

"Sounds good to me," Becky said, snuggling closer to her new husband and grinning at her embarrassed brother. "So, any plans along those lines, Cody? Any prospects?"

The ensuing silence was almost palpable. Becky had invited a few of the unmarried members of her ladies' Sunday school class to join them that evening. Those women were especially interested in hearing her brother's answer. When he said, "Yes," their sighs were audible.

Becky shrugged. "Oh, well. I tried." She looked to Logan, her gaze filled with tenderness and adoration. "I wish everyone as much happiness as we've found."

"And a blessed Christmas," he added, "the first of many to come."

* * * * *

Look for Valerie Hansen in the
Faith at the Crossroads series with
THE DANGER WITHIN,
coming in February 2006
only from Love Inspired Suspense!

Dear Reader,

It's easy to say we're walking by faith when everything in life is going our way, yet it's those other times, the harder times, when we need to focus most on trusting God.

No matter how bleak things look, we aren't alone in our troubles if we've given our lives to Christ. I don't have the answer to why bad things happen. Nobody does. But I do know that God has been with me through many trials and that every time I trust Him completely, I grow stronger in my faith. It's always easier to look back and see the handiwork of God than it is to step into an unknown future unafraid. But that's when we most need to do just that.

The characters and stories I create are meant to convey a sense of the joy—and of the problems—we believers share. If you belong to Him, trust Him. If you're questioning whether or not you're truly His child, all you have to do is surrender your pride, ask Jesus to forgive and accept you right now, and He will. It's that easy.

I love to hear from readers. The quickest replies are by e-mail—VALW@CENTURYTEL.NET—or you can write to me at P.O. Box 13, Glencoe, AR, 72539 and I'll do my best to answer as soon as I can. www.centurytel.net/valeriewhisenand/ will take you to my Web site.

Blessings,

Valerie Hansen

SUGAR PLUMS FOR DRY CREEK

BY

JANET TRONSTAD

Judd Bowman wanted to give his young cousins, whom
he was raising, a Christmas to remember. Being part
of Dry Creek's first *Nutcracker* production was the one
thing they wanted. Yet when Judd met Lizette Baker, the
ballet teacher, he discovered he had a wish of his own:
to have Lizette by his side for the rest of their lives....

Don't miss SUGAR PLUMS FOR DRY CREEK
On sale December 2005

Available at your favorite retail outlet.

LARGER PRINT BOOKS!

2 FREE LARGER PRINT NOVELS PLUS A FREE MYSTERY GIFT

Love Inspired®

Larger print novels are now available...

YES! Please send me 2 FREE LARGER PRINT Love Inspired® novels and my FREE mystery gift. After receiving them, if I don't wish to receive any more books, I can return the shipping statement marked "cancel." If I don't cancel, I will receive 4 brand-new novels every month and be billed just $4.24 per book in the U.S., or $4.99 per book in Canada, plus 25¢ shipping and handling per book and applicable taxes, if any*. That's a savings of over 20% off the cover price! I understand that accepting the 2 free books and gift places me under no obligation to buy anything. I can always return a shipment and cancel at any time. Even if I never buy another book from Steeple Hill, the two free books and gift are mine to keep forever.

121 IDN D733 321 IDN D74F

Name		(PLEASE PRINT)	
Address			Apt.
City	State/Prov.		Zip/Postal Code

Signature (if under 18, a parent or guardian must sign)

Order online at www.LoveInspiredBooks.com

Or mail to Steeple Hill Reader Service™:

IN U.S.A.	IN CANADA
3010 Walden Ave.	P.O. Box 609
P.O. Box 1867	Fort Erie, Ontario
Buffalo, NY 14240-1867	L2A 5X3

Are you a current Love Inspired subscriber and want to receive the larger print edition?

Call 1-800-221-5011 today!

* Terms and prices subject to change without notice. NY residents add applicable sales tax. Canadian residents will be charged applicable provincial taxes and GST. This offer is limited to one order per household. All orders subject to approval. Credit or debit balances in a customer's account(s) may be offset by any other outstanding balance owed by or to the customer.

LILPO05

Love Inspired®

SUSPENSE

TITL~~E~~ MONTH

Don't ~~...~~ ~~...~~ber

SOU~~...~~
Texa~~...~~
Whe~~...~~ a
deaf~~...~~ ~~...~~xican
orph~~...~~
Isabe~~...~~
care,~~...~~
out t~~...~~

YULE~~...~~
When~~...~~ ~~...~~ved
into t~~...~~
follow~~...~~
the "p~~...~~
protec~~...~~

LISCNM1105